*Winner of the 37th Annual
3-Day Novel Writing Contest . . .*

TRAVERSING LEONARD

BY *Craig Savel*

*Winner of the 37th Annual 3-Day
Novel Writing Contest*

ANVIL PRESS / CANADA

Copyright © 2015 by Craig Savel

All rights reserved. No part of this book may be reproduced by any means without the prior written permission of the publisher, with the exception of brief passages in reviews. Any request for photocopying or other reprographic copying of any part of this book must be directed in writing to access: The Canadian Copyright Licensing Agency, One Yonge Street, Suite 800, Toronto, Ontario, Canada, M5E 1E5.

LIBRARY AND ARCHIVES CANADA CATALOGUING IN PUBLICATION

Savel, Craig, author
    Traversing Leonard / Craig Savel. – First edition.

ISBN 978-1-77214-033-0 (paperback)

    I. Title.

PS3619.A94T73 2015   813'.6   C2015-905980-1

Printed and bound in Canada
Cover design by Derek von Essen
Interior by HeimatHouse
Represented in Canada by the Publishers Group Canada
Distributed by Raincoast Books

The publisher gratefully acknowledges the financial assistance of the Canada Council for the Arts, the Government of Canada through the Canada Book Fund, and the Province of British Columbia through the B.C. Arts Council and the Book Publishing Tax Credit.

Anvil Press Publishers Inc.
P.O. Box 3008, Main Post Office
Vancouver, B.C. V6B 3X5 CANADA
www.anvilpress.com

To my wonderful wife, Marion Stein,
the better craftswoman in everything!

AVANT LA DELUGE

He's in my room. I can hear him. I can smell his breath. I know that he had a bagel with cream cheese and lox for breakfast. His hygiene isn't what most people's sense of personal cleanliness is. But then again, why should it be? I've never known him to have friends, to get laid. He knows only three things: math, physics, and how to be really annoying.

"Leonard, what do you want?" I ask, the beginning and end punctuated with stage sighs hoping he will get the hint. I realize it is the same voice I used to use for my ex-girlfriend's cat, who used to paw me awake at five in the morning for kibble.

That was how it started and I wished I had listened to whatever executive function I had in my brain and kicked his ass out onto Broadway. But I felt sorry for the old man and he had no place to go. Leonard Zavitsky was a legend in the physics community. Even after he had become a washed-up disgrace, he was still an awe-inspiring presence. I had been around academia for a while. I knew how stupid, petty, and venal the smartest of the smartest were. When he talked of a conspiracy because he wasn't a "team player" I was not one to disagree. When my faculty mentor told me that spending too much time with that guy—"I don't even fucking know if he is on faculty" was what he said—would not be a help in any tenure-track trophy, I should have listened, but instead some sense of justice made me allow him to be a part of my life.

"Young man," he began with his combination of Brooklyn and newscaster voice that made me laugh. He almost always called me "young man" instead of Paul. I was only Paul when he was angry with me.

"Young man, I need to know if you are truly serious about what we discussed last night. You know that I don't have the technological experience of the younger generation, but—well apart from that incident for which I am *persona non grata* in the campus—you know that I would be the one heading this department, even acting as your mentor and faculty advisor. You know that I am right."

I don't think he realized how that voice gave the impression of someone who wanted to be more than he was, but that was Leonard. The first time I met him, I thought he was a janitor or something. He had white hair at every angle, a paunch, and he didn't bathe much. Colleagues joked about the Leonard Condensate, one whiff of which reduced matter into muck. He stuffed newspapers in his pockets to read on his ramblings in Upper Manhattan. He never took the subway, only walked. Nobody knew where he slept. Many people in the department at Columbia weren't even sure if he was still drawing a salary. The truth was that some older professors, now doddering emerituses or emerita or whatever, still had feelings for Leonard and thought that his transgressions, while great, didn't cancel out his genuine work as a young man. He could at least get a job as a custodian, which is what he, in fact, was. I don't think he ever pushed a broom in his life but it was a place for him to go to and be annoying, and also a place for him to swoop in and make real contributions to physics. Mostly he either hung around the library and cadged invitations to various laboratories or roamed the famous tunnels under the campus. Once in the dead of winter he even went up to Lamont-Doherty, the geology lab which is up in Rockland County. He walked there.

"Leonard, I am not sure I can do that. Knowing you has already put me in deep shit with the head of the department. He wants to know why I am…"

"Hanging around with a doddering old fool who faked numbers on his research and traverses the tunnels beneath the university to break into classrooms, right?"

"Well, yes, although I know you are a genius."

"Don't patronize me, Paul!"

"I'm not."

"Young man, you know I have an Erdős number of 1. You know that I birthed the quantum many-worlds hypothesis, do you not? Those numbers weren't faked. They may have been estimated a bit but it was merely an inadvertent error. We didn't have fancy word processors in those days. Any error was simply carelessness. I will only admit to sloppiness."

"Yes, Leonard, you and Erdős were tight bros."

"Tight what? I don't understand the argot of you young idiots. Young man, frankly, I am a bit personally hurt by your attacks. Erdős knew I was right. He and I used to take amphetamines and talk math for days non-stop. It was a transcendent experience. You young people think you invented performance-enhancing drugs? You did not. We knew, Paul, *we knew* that with the correct management of an electromagnetic field, the advanced technology that we didn't have in those days, and, a bit of luck, we could theoretically traverse the quantum universes, an infinitude of universes like bubbles on a string."

"Erdős was a mathematician, not a physicist, he was pure math. Did he even know what string theory or quantum bubbles were?"

He went on as if he didn't even consider what I just said.

"And how would we manage that field? All it would take is a Faraday cage, and some precise measurement equipment, of the type we simply did not have in my younger days, young man."

I realized I had to go to the bathroom but I was naked, and here was Leonard sitting on the end of my bed, breathing heavily the odour of a good old Upper West Side Jewish breakfast of the kind you actually can't get on the Upper West Side anymore. Long Island memories flooded into me. Most of them were not good. I had fled the 'burbs and the LIRR and the big hair. I wasn't going back.

Leonard wasn't going to move, I had to piss. Oh well, I doubted he'd even notice my nakedness and I don't think he had a sexual thought in his life—a true math monk.

I jumped up naked and made for the bathroom.

"Leonard, I have to pee. I'll be right back."

"Of course, young man, I know how I am inconveniencing you. But let me continue. And how will we encode the information so that the obligate randomness which is inherent in quantum entanglement, and that is mandated by both theory and experiment, can be overcome?"

My nakedness and the fact that I was using the toilet didn't seem to faze Leonard. I also knew that Leonard used the toilet because there was piss all over the seat and on the floor.

"Damn Leonard, can't you lift up the seat to pee, and aim? I mean, there's piss all over the floor!"

"I am sorry, young man, but when you are as old as I am the prostate plays cruel jokes on you. You'll see."

"You could still clean up after yourself."

"I will, of course, I will, but let's talk about formulae. I know we can solve this."

"*Formulas* Leonard, 'formulae' sounds ridiculous, even scientists don't talk like that nowadays. You don't call two stadiums 'stadia' do you?"

"I do, young man, of course I do, what else would you call them?"

I went back to my bedroom to put on cargo pants and a T-shirt, all the while Leonard tailing me. I resolved, or rather I should have resolved, to kick him out right there. His legendary annoying qualities weren't charming anymore. He wasn't the old eccentric you tell friends about. This wasn't *Tuesdays with Morrie*, but rather some old former genius ranting about time travel and quantum information signalling and quantum teleportation into alternate realities. The "spooky action at a distance" Einstein couldn't abide. Yet I knew that in theory Leonard's idea was solid. The math was correct. I was doing similar research myself.

"Leonard, look, I have to go, you can stay here, but please

let me go and do my work. We can talk tonight. I promise." Leonard deflated as he always did, his small pot-belly sagged more than it usually did and his white hair seemed to move on its own to flow over his forehead. I deflated him but he responded with a quick OK. I started to give him a spare key, but then he stopped me.

"No need, young man; there isn't a lock in this world that I can't pick."

I sighed and left, hoping that the apartment would still be in some order of cleanliness when I returned. I didn't know what Leonard would do all day. It was a weekend. Perhaps walk Central Park or Morningside Park looking at trees. Or perhaps he played the licence plate game where he would walk and walk and only stop when enough out-of-state licence plates were identified. Leonard had his obsessions, but when it came to pure science, he was also ahead of his time.

Later that day in the lab, I was going over the results of one of the experiments we were doing. It was a rather simple one and I was surprised it was never attempted before. The idea of quantum entanglement, which means, basically, that changing the aspect of one photon's wave function instantaneously changes another. It was settled after Alain Aspect's 1982 experiment. This was not necessarily proof of instantaneous information travel, according to Bell's theorem. A person reading some of the work of Kurakin, especially "Hidden variables and hidden time in quantum theory" will see how the physical reality of the Aspect experiment does not contradict anything else in quantum physics. My first paper with Slava Mishkin shows how there is a hidden order in some of the random quantum matrices generated, and that it is in fact pseudo-random. That was the theory. That was *my* theory and I wanted to apply it to something real and practical. I knew, and my advisor did too, that if you concentrate two slightly differing sorts of finely calibrated lasers in such a way that their wave heights cancel each other out, you can collapse the wave function of many particles at once, causing a sort of chain reaction. You can theoretically impose order and, most importantly, encode information into the strange quantum world. The problem is that there was never a way to calibrate lasers and control light perfectly. It wasn't just a matter of slowing photons down. It was getting rid of all the noise so that only the information encoded was transmitted. We had the idea of building a massive Faraday cage, deep into the Manhattan schist, buried below the sub-basement of the Engineering Building. Even though it was one of the most crowded cities on earth, this would have a shielding effect, making sure there was no background noise to mess up the photons. This also meant we could introduce our pseudo background noise. We could control what was "random." We were building on Aspect's experiment.

It was rough going. I resented having to do this in Manhattan where you're never more than a block away from a subway line. Some of Columbia's rural campuses which were dedicated to science would be a more practical setting. We had to be very secret about this work. Much of it was Department of Defense-funded. They felt that we were actually less conspicuous in a crowded city like New York. This meant, however, we could never get the background electromagnetism—even inside a Faraday cage—to reduce true random noise to zero. A person can make a Faraday cage from wires, aluminum foil and a few other things but we needed more than that to just cancel out cellphone signals. We needed absolute electromagnetic quiet. We desperately needed to show that, in some fashion, in the real world, we could make the "spooky action at a distance" of the Aspect experiment controllable and not-random. If we could do that, a whole new world of quantum computing could open up. The math was difficult, basically a lot of matrix mechanics with a lot of number-crunching, and the numbers only worked out if you used imaginary numbers. We knew we could rely on computers to do the math if we only had the correct model. Once we had that we could build a perfect Faraday cage, and quantumly cancel out any random noise we wanted and prove that the spooky action at a distance effect could be controlled—and information passed—with a minimum of energy. I dreamed this hypothesis along with Leonard, something I kept quiet, but here I admit that it was Leonard's theory, as crazy as it was. All I did was translate it into math that people could understand, at least that people with a math and physics background could understand.

Alain Aspect once came to campus and we briefed him on our findings. We took him out to a restaurant in Little Senegal, in Harlem, not far from the Columbia campus. Someone noted that Aspect had spent time in West Africa. The dinner started off well, with great talk about theoretical physics and, of course, the requisite grousing about campus politics. There was a ngoni player from Mali and the slow tuneful playing lent an air of warmth to the dinner. But of course Leonard found out and invited himself along. Nobody but me knew that the work I was doing was Leonard's work. Leonard was now a custodian so that was the way it was. I knew that Leonard didn't accept it, but it was the best that he could hope for.

In crowds like this, Leonard liked to needle me about my supposedly effete ways. Of course when I asked for something vegetarian Leonard said to the waiter, *"L'agneau, c'est formidable, mais mon mec, le Toubab? Il est vegetarian. Il mange pas de viands, pas des oiseaus, pas de poulet. Avez vous, je ne sais pas, fonio avec des legumes."* He was showing off his semi-grammatical French to the crowd. He then began to talk to Aspect non-stop in French, preventing anyone else from joining the discussion. Who knows what they were talking about? Aspect got up, excused himself, and said in English to the chief of the department, "I've got to get the fuck out of here."

And that was that. The great French quantum physicist whose work we were building on ran away from us because of Leonard. The ngoni player was playing a truly mournful song now. It matched my feelings.

I was thinking about this because, fundamentally, as I said, Leonard's math was sound. It might have been the only sound part of his entire being.

We had decided to build a theoretical model. If it held we'd get more funding from the Department of Defense to build a bigger Faraday cage and get more powerful lasers. Maybe even in a place where you don't have to worry about the rumblings of a subway train disrupting your earth-shaking, very expensive, incredibly complex experiment. We had the perfect backstory for funding. Everything had to have a backstory today. We had gotten some money from the Department of

Defense but not enough to build the kind of cage we needed. We figured, with the model, we could at least perform a "proof-of-concept" experiment proving our model worked. Then we figured we would get funding to build the cage we needed. We were planning to tell the DoD that it was a perfect model for people control. We could create a world of happy contented drones. They'd eat that up.

I wasn't making progress with my work and decided to take a walk. I didn't want to go home because I really didn't know if Leonard had cleared out and I needed some Leonard-free time. It was a beautiful autumn day and from Leonard, of course, I knew where the best fall color in Central Park and Morningside Park was. I walked down toward Morningside Drive; I always loved how from the drive you can look over Harlem and Morningside Park all the way to Queens. It seemed almost un-New York-like. I loved how families barbecued, children played games, people walked their dogs and the city didn't seem so overwhelming. I began to recognize people, the landscape, every turtle, duck, and egret in the lake. I recognized and nodded to the older woman with her pet pot-bellied pig, out for a walk. I stood over the wall to look down at the park and felt myself calm. Because I really did have to go back and was famished, I began to head back to the campus. On the walk, I found myself noticing licence plates. Just then I spotted one. Idaho. I read that it said FAMOUS POTATOES. In spite of myself I was excited. You don't see too many Idaho licence plates on cars in New York.

I stopped in the middle of 116th Street, a block from the drive, and almost got hit by a cyclist. That annoying habit of

Leonard had now infected me. I didn't have much in my life. My only girlfriend had left me. I wasn't particularly handsome or at ease with women. My family thought I was wasting my life when I could've gone to Silicon Valley and become a zillionaire. Every time there was an article in a magazine about some mathematician or physicist who went to Wall Street and now had a fleet of private jets I would get the "phone call." My father would ask me what I was doing with my life. I had no idea but I couldn't imagine myself on a trading floor in a fiery red power tie.

The only thing I did have was my mind and my science. I only felt truly alive when I was thinking of the universe, the reality of it and how it was built. I thought sometimes that it was some sort of strange holographic vision. It almost made me religious! I thought numbers and math were the universal language of God, if there was such a thing. I could see why people got mystical and how new age people threw quantum theory into their conversation. Of course they hadn't the slightest clue of what they were talking about, but the truth was even more mind-blowing and, frankly, far more mystical than anything that they could conceive of. I was a scientist. Science was one small place in my world where I didn't feel like I was part of the scenery. I actually had things to say and people listened. My grandfather used to call some people "big *machers*," sort of Yiddish for big shots. I'd never be a big *macher*, but here I was at least a small to medium *macher*. There was no way I was going to become a crazy sexless math crank that walked around Manhattan checking for cars with out-of-state licence plates, delighted when he spotted a rare one.

I decided right then and there that Leonard Zavitsky had to

leave my life. I was going to take a walk in the park, go back to the lab, try to crunch some numbers and then kick Leonard out. I know he can pick locks but he can't pick all of them. If he broke into my apartment to sleep, I'd call the cops. I didn't need this.

I made my way back to Columbia, stopping at the Pear Tree Market on Amsterdam. I got my usual smoky tofu sandwich and gave my usual dollar to the homeless drunk who sat in front of the deli. He was my drunk and we usually chatted for about five minutes. I don't know why we struck up a relationship of sorts but it had lasted my entire time at Columbia.

Today he looked at me and said, "Listen young fellah, time ain't nothing but bullshit, and this universe of ours ain't nothing but someone else's memory. You know what I'm sayin'? Sometimes I feel like none of this is real? You see what I'm sayin'? That's why I drink."

A short pause and then he said, "God bless you and Jesus is gonna bless you."

I laughed, but inside I wasn't. When I first met Leonard and he talked to me about how we can traverse quantum bubbles I asked him how that would work.

"If that is the case then why don't we see strangers from different universes who are like us but not like us? Why don't we see someone who commented on what a great painter Hitler was, and never knew what he became in our quantum universe because in that person's universe Hitler was only a great painter—maybe he hated Jews privately, but the Hitler that we knew never existed."

"But we see that every day, young man, we call it schizophrenia, madness, creativity, or visions."

I looked at him skeptically and twirled my hair. I was in a phase when I had very long hair.

"Young man, don't forget the quantum pseudo-randomness of what we speak will only allow us to traverse the string one at a time. The further away you go, the more energy needed, the more noise needs to be filtered and the harder it gets to traverse. If our theory, *my theory*, is correct we can only peek into the universe of our neighbours. You know that déjà vu feeling? What do you think it is?"

"Random electrons firing in neurons? I don't know. I'm not a neuroscientist. But I am a physicist and you are talking like some pseudoscientific nut."

"OK, believe what you want professor longhair."

I got my hair cut the next day. As drawn as I was to Leonard, he annoyed me so that if he mentioned my hair it had to go. Strangely, with short hair, I noticed that people began to take me more seriously.

"Jesus is gonna bless you young fellah and you know what else?"

I had forgotten I was next to the homeless man, he was holding my hand and looking me straight in the eye.

"I don't know where I been or where I am going but I gotta go home. This isn't home to me, nothing is right, that is when I began drinking. Son, you know where everything is the same but it ain't? They said I was crazy, but you a good man. Am I crazy?"

"Hell no, you're not crazy, no more crazy than anyone else, and God bless you too."

We hugged each other. Hugged each other tight. And I swear

I saw a tear shed from his eye. A single tear leave the corner of his eye and fall to the ground.

Finally he said "L'chaim brother. Jesus gonna come for us," and gave me the thumbs up sign. I had no idea if he knew I was Jewish. He talked to me about Jesus all the time.

I laughed, came a quantum tear. I knew that the emotion of the moment got to me but that that was all it was, there was no random rip in the quantum fabric. My friend wasn't from a different bubble universe, he was just a drunk down on his luck. Yet when I hugged him, and saw that tear fall from his face, I knew deep down that Leonard was right. I also knew that if he was right then reality itself was malleable and illusory. It is no wonder Leonard walks around Upper Manhattan muttering and checking for out-of-state licence plates. It's no wonder this guy drinks to forget. He drinks to forget that he doesn't exist. I don't exist. Nobody exists.

Back at the lab I ate my smoky tofu at my desk. Hundreds of lines of code were streaming across my screen. I enjoyed looking at it. It was old school but it sort of inspired me. I even set up my workstation to have a blue screen background and a blinking cursor.

I went back to work. I entered the Zavitsky formula, although I knew I couldn't call it that and watched the screen go to work. The randomness was, to me, beautiful. I knew that there was a hidden order, a true pattern in the randomness, and once we got it we could calibrate the lasers and encode information and transmit it instantly. I got up to stretch my legs and look out the window.

My lab was not in Pupin Hall, where the rest of the physics

department was located. I was in Mudd Hall where applied engineering was. I was ensconced in Mudd because of military secrecy, even though everyone in Pupin and Mudd knew exactly what I was doing. Mudd was considered the ugliest building on campus, but to me it was home. My lab looked out not over the leafy campus, nor Broadway, but Amsterdam—north of that ugly walkway over Amsterdam that Columbia built in the fifties. You could practically smell the piss from generations of drunken fratboys and homeless men right from my office. I saw a single street tree, a honey locust in all its beautiful golden autumn glory. A honey locust without thorns in case some freshman accidentally staggered into it. I remember thinking, That tree is Leonard! Out of place and out of time and out of thorns.

Would Leonard Zavitsky never be out of my life? I had to cut him loose. I was on the verge of great research and even though he started the thought train, he was just too crazy, too all-consuming, too much of an emotional vampire for me to handle. It's one thing to encode information and to transmit it across distances instantly. It's one thing even to think of the universe as one of many bubbles along a cosmic quantum string. It's another thing entirely to build a machine to transmit people across time instantly. That's where science ends and craziness begins. That's where my career ends and my new career selling gadgets in a department store out on Long Island begins. No way that was gonna happen.

Funny thing was, when I got home Leonard had in fact left; the apartment was clean and there was even food in the fridge. I was relieved, but also saddened. The number-crunching that day didn't go well. The problem was that you had to block out all stray electromagnetism and randomness, but then introduce phony randomness, pseudo-randomness we call it, but you can't fool reality. What might be random to a human is anything but to the universe, and the universe was not amused. Our experiment was a dud and for the first time I felt that we were going down a blind alley. Spooky action at a distance might be truly random forever and that was it. I went to sleep.

Came Sunday and another brilliant autumn day. I couldn't concentrate on science. I was lonely and horny. It had been two years since Maria left me and besides my right hand, I hadn't had a sex partner. Frankly, I felt pathetic. I missed Maria, but I didn't miss her anger or her tirades. Frankly, for me it was physical. She was a beautiful Colombian, and she chose me. Most of the few women in my life chose me because I wouldn't have had the guts to pursue them. She finally left me for a carpenter with huge muscles. I think I bored her and I had no idea how to deal with the real world. I picked up the phone, almost ready to call her, realized the futility, and realized I didn't have a single friend in the world. My existence was so lonely, so monastic, I was going crazy. I wished that for just one night I could be a frat boy in a bar and feign interest in whatever sports team was on the TV.

Not for the first time I felt like Leonard, an outcast from life. Even amongst my colleagues, if it wasn't work-related, I had no idea how to talk to people, how to communicate with them. No wonder I got put in Mudd.

I basically stayed in bed and then went to the Pear Tree for some more smoky tofu, and maybe a black and white cookie.

There was a crowd in front of the deli. Three cop cars, EMS and yellow tape.

"What happened?" I asked a beautiful young Indian American woman wearing short shorts despite the October temps.

"Um, like I think this homeless guy killed himself."

Then I saw him, my homeless guy lying in front of his crate. He used a razor to slash his wrists and did a good job of it. He knew exactly how to kill himself quickly. He opened his artery lengthwise from wrist to lower arm—rather than across his wrists—so the entire artery opened. There was almost no chance to save him. He lay in front of his crate with a beautiful smile. He was at peace, finally.

"Um, like gross, he had to do it right on the street?" My princess stifled a laugh. Some young, well-muscled guy with a blond crewcut, in shorts and a T-shirt—again, despite it being October—stepped up and decided to take a selfie in front of the body. His buddies were egging him on. A cop and an EMS person said at the same time, "What the fuck, buddy?" And the cop pushed him away.

He said something about police brutality and the cop just looked at him. I was actually hoping for a little NYPD whoop-ass, but I also knew that white kids going to Ivy League schools were generally immune from police brutality. The young frat boy lost his nerve and slowly left the crowd, brushing by me. I said to him, "You know he was a person, a human being. He couldn't have been happy. Was it really so important to get a pic with him?"

"Suck my dick, asshole!" he said, to twitters from the crowd, including my beautiful Indian princess in short shorts. And he walked on.

"I fucking knew him, he was a person!" I yelled at his back. I started to walk away, my appetite finished. I felt a tap on my back and it was the cop who had pushed the kid away.

"Did you know him? What was his name? We don't have any ID. Did he have next of kin? You could really help us out. Do you know why he might want to off himself?"

I was embarrassed. I felt so good about myself for talking to this guy for years and giving him money and I didn't even know his name. How close could we really have been?

"Um, no officer, you see, he would hang out there and I'd buy him coffee and give him money and we'd chat a bit, that was all. But he was a human being. He had his problems, but you know, he cared. He just never felt at home anywhere, like he was floating in a different universe. It drove him crazy. Every day he told me that Jesus would save me. Jesus didn't save him, did he?"

The cop thanked me and I could feel his eyes rolling even though they didn't. I wasted his time. The frat boy wasted his time, this homeless guy wasted his time. Time was a waste.

ENTROPY IS NOT A WASTE

Suddenly I realized I had got it. Leonard was a visionary. The homeless guy (I later found out everyone called him Red) was a visionary. William Butler Yeats in that poem that goes "Things fall apart; the centre cannot hold" was a visionary. That was the whole point of everything. That was the answer to my problem. Things always fell apart. The centre will never hold, in the quantum world and in the real world. Information degrades the more you transmit it because of random background effects. That is information entropy. Claude Shannon discovered that, became famous, and then used it to win big on the stock market and in Las Vegas. He was sixty years ahead of his time. What I had to do was introduce some redundancy into my pseudo-randmoness and allow for some true randomness. Because my information is redundant, it's lossy. That means it can be retrieved. Using Shannon's theorem you can still get the information back. You didn't have to make sure every bit of background noise was gone. I was halfway there!

I went back home, jerked off, and fell asleep. Monday was going to be a great day!

Monday wasn't so great a day after all. I was famished and yet since I led such a monastic existence, I had to go to the Pear Tree for breakfast. The box where Red sat was still there, his blood stains had been washed away but it was a poor job. The blood now merged with the general grime of New York. A bouquet of flowers and a note was on top of the box. "Goodbye Red, we always will love you," read the note. It was signed, staff of the Pear Tree.

In the deli, beside the counter there was a little box, what my grandparents would call a *pushke,* for contributions to Red's funeral, along with a picture of Red smiling his toothless grin on his box in front of the Pear Tree. It seems that Red was from Georgia and had an ex-wife he still kept in contact with. The money was for his funeral and transport back down to Georgia. I kept staring at Red's picture, looking into his eyes, searching for an answer, but any secrets Red had he took with him. I put twenty dollars in the box and forgot my egg sandwich. By the time I got to the lab I was famished. I didn't want to go back to the Pear Tree—not that day, possibly never again. I grabbed a muffin from the cart in front of the lab and went to my office. The inevitable sugar crash was upon me and I was cranky when my advisor walked in.

"How'd it go this weekend?"

"Well, Dave," I began, "I am not making any progress at all. To tell you the truth, I am fucking stuck! I'm wondering if we've made a big mistake in even attempting this. The theoretical physics is correct but theoretical doesn't get the grant money, does it? We can't take the physics and math and do shit with it can we?"

Dave laughed. Only a few friends and colleagues called him Dave, even though he insisted everyone did. He would only gently correct a person who called him Davidson instead of the correct Davisson. His full name was Davisson Steven Chambliss IV and he was a scion of the Chambliss dynasty. The Chamblisses and the Davissons were the cream of U.S. society. When his cousin married a Rockefeller most of the family considered it a step down. When another cousin married into the British nobility, it was a step up for the nobles. One could say that he was the sort of old money WASP for whom the Ivy League was built, although he tried earnestly not to show it. Rather, he tried much too hard to affect a lower-class air. He cursed like a drunken sailor and loved it when his students did too. I sometimes had to dirty up my speech. It didn't help mask his privileged upbringing since he still talked with what was called Connecticut lockjaw and still sounded a bit like Thurston Howell from *Gilligan's Island*. His cursing only seemed to draw even more attention to his upper-crust background. He usually padded around in Converse high-top sneakers, jeans and T-shirts, but I still always imagined him with a pipe and one of those tweed jackets with padded elbows, even though I had no idea if true WASPs actually wore those.

"Yesterday you sent me a gushing email about how you figured things out. Now you're stuck? OK Pavel, let me guess, that old coot's formulas, no, *formulae*, are getting in your way."

"No, I..."

Dave cut me off. He was the only person who I could stand to call me by my given name instead of Paul.

"Pavel, listen, I know he was once a genius, I know he can

be entertaining, but he is fucking crazy—a basket case. I know you don't want to hurt the guy but don't let him bring you down. I get more coherent theories from crazy fuckers from trailer parks who are convinced they've proven that the Bible predicts that the current president is the spawn of Satan or some shit or another. You'll never get past this problem, and we'll never get any more grant money from the defense department if you let him into your head, into your life."

"Dave, come on. I know he's nuts but he isn't an idiot. You yourself know he's a genius."

"*Was* Pavel, was. I am talking past tense. If I could set him up as body odour emeritus or fartmaster to the physics department or some court jester, I would. I feel bad for the guy. Enough money is pissed away to find something for him. They found a minor fuck-up in his thesis twenty-five years after he's on faculty and they crucified him for it. Who knows what he might have accomplished by now. That wasn't right, downright, fucking vindictive, but it happened. It isn't our fault it made him bat-shit bonkers."

"Dave, I..."

"Pavel, he stinks to high heaven. He doesn't brush his teeth. He annoys people. He's a distraction."

"I know, but..."

"We can't afford distractions. My ass is on the line too, you know. This entire project was speculative and the stink of Leonard Zavitsky already permeates this project in a lot of people's minds. The department head thinks this whole project is a monumental piss of money. Engineering wonders why they have to give space to the physics department in their godforsaken Stalinist shithole. I am sorry. If he comes around, I don't want him in the lab, I don't want him bothering you. If he comes, we call security and have him escorted. I'm sorry."

I looked at him, angry now, "The department head thinks this is a monumental piss of money? Jeez, you know what he pisses away on junkets to conferences which happen to always be in exotic locations?"

"Pavel, I know, but he's head of department, he can piss wherever he wants to. We can't. That is reality. You may wish it is not but it is, and it's probably the same in whatever quantum bubble your friend wants to traipse in."

I stared at him.

"Sorry, Pavel, I thought that was funny. You've got to cut him from your life. Do you want to be some sexless old crazy guy running around the campus collecting acorns?"

"He's harmless."

"He's not intentionally harmful but he's harming you. Your career."

Dave stared at me hard and put his long elegant fingers on my shoulders and said: "Pavel, trust me on this. Cut him loose. Save yourself."

I wish I had had the courage to respond with some cutting remark. I wish that I had made some speech defending the true geniuses who might appear to be crazy to the world. I didn't. I didn't know what to say, didn't think of anything to say until later. *L'esprit de l'escalier* the French call it. All I said was, "OK Dave, don't worry about me, I won't let you down."

"Thank fucking God!" he proclaimed in an even more pronounced upper-class New England Brahmin accent. I had to suppress a laugh at that. Sometimes I think Dave cursed so much because the mix of four-letter words and his upper-crust accent disarmed people so easily.

I still had the problem, but the germ of the solution. I started to tell Dave that but then stopped. It seemed like the solution was a secret shared by me, Leonard, and Red. We were in our own ways three outcasts in the world, never to be stars. It was our secret. Maybe I'd even add Red as a co-author once I wrote the paper.

A lot of dull number-crunching lay ahead before I revised the formula to create what I was calling pseudo-random degradable entropy matrices. I figured that sounded both unintelligible and impressive enough for any funder. I also knew that this was a way to traverse the bubbles, just like Leonard had said. We could time travel. We could be quantumnauts, just like Leonard had said. And even if we couldn't, I knew that I could make a lot of money with this, since it was a way to encode information securely, which was the public face of my research. Hell, maybe there would even be an article about me.

I had been trying to figure this out all afternoon when Leonard, of course Leonard, walked into a classroom with a broom—he was a custodian after all. Leonard let the broom fall down so it made a huge noise. He picked up a marker and stared at the wall and began to write equations on it. Soon he drew a crowd and the class that was scheduled for that room was moved. Leonard, legendary Leonard, could always draw a crowd. Even those who hated him admired his genius for math. I noticed that Dave was stretching his tall, angular, almost feminine neck to see what Leonard was writing.

After he finished writing the equations, he threw down the marker and turned and said, "Here it is people! Proof that with redundancy you can create true guided randomness that has all the characteristics of pseudo-randomness when you want it but can also be truly random. Do you realize, gentlemen, and ladies, what this means?"

A few titters from the assembled group.

Dave finally said, "Leonard, I have no idea what the fuck this means."

"Mr. Chambliss," Leonard said pointedly, "this means quantum teleportation through time, if only you can build a cage that can block out all external random noise."

A few nervous twitters emanated from the crowd. Dave gave a stage laugh that dripped with sarcasm. "Leonard," he said, "your ideas are interesting, intriguing really. I owe Pavel an apology, he's been hanging around you and I dare say that your ideas can help us solve the specific problems we're working on. We can use this to make pseudo-random random."

Leonard was glowing. Just then he let out an audible fart.

"But that is it. We can use this to transmit information in discrete packets over distance instantaneously. We can't use it to transmit ourselves anywhere except for the loony bin. We're scientists. We deal in reality. If we want to deal in quantum time travel, or whatever, then we ought to move to the English department and write science fiction."

"What is science fiction but science that hasn't been invented yet?" asked Leonard.

"Leonard, that is great line but I prefer my science fiction with a lot of science fiction sex scenes. Thank you, but now it is time for this department to get back to work. Pavel, if you will, let's talk about this, and Leonard, you will get full credit as a collaborator."

"Why, thank you so much Mr. Chambliss, thank you ever so much."

Now it was Leonard's turn for sarcasm.

Dave just muttered a "you are welcome" and was about to ask Leonard to leave. But he turned and did a curious thing. He put a hand on Leonard's shoulder and said simply, "Stay."

Leonard stayed.

Three weeks—no, four weeks later—I was working in the lab. It was cold because the college turns the heat down on weekends and it is now mid-November. Even with a sweater and scarf it's freezing. I run my program through our computer grid again and try the experiment again. The two lasers are finely calibrated to fire one photon at a time. One laser is to fire in a random pattern that encodes redundant pseudo-random patterns. If all goes well. Well, if all goes well we've just transported information instantly across distances, essentially collapsing time.

I knew it wasn't going to work, there is too much noise. Even though we are below ground, inside our makeshift Faraday cage, with Manhattan schist all around us, some noise is getting in. I suddenly hear a bang as the boiler kicks off entirely. Now no heat. In an hour it will be down to the forties in my cave. I went to the Pear Tree and grabbed some food. Even at three in the morning it was crowded. In front of me in the checkout line two students were energetically kissing each other while one handed out a credit card to pay for the night's beer. I wanted to shout, "Get a room!"

"Everyone's in love," the man behind the counter told me when it was my turn.

"Everyone but me," I said, and took my vegan whatever and potato chips back to the lab.

I decided to rerun the program and desultorily ate my lunch at three in the morning.

The experiment worked! It fucking worked. I realized that whatever background noise existed was background infrared radiation from the heat. Once the boiler was turned off and it was cold enough, the radiation was not a problem. Leonard's math works, it just has to be really cold. I ran the teleportation experiment again, slowing down each laser, but changing the order in the first one. The second one responded INSTANTLY. It would appear faster than light but it was not speed, but time that was being warped. We had done it. I wanted to tell Dave. I wanted to tell Leonard. I could already imagine myself on important panels telling the president what I think about some important issue involving big science.

PHASE TRANSITION

I should've stopped there. I'd have written a paper with Dave. We'd get criticism. It would play out in the science journals, sure, but I knew the science would hold up. We'd get the grant and try to refine the theory so that quantum information could have real world application. "Science for good" I called it.

Leonard's siren song put an end to that.

After Dave let him stay, Leonard lived in various rooms in Columbia. He probably had a secret apartment in the tunnels below campus somewhere. I finally told him he could come back to my place on two conditions: he bathed regularly and he changed his underwear every day. He grumpily acceded to my demands as if I had asked him to be a eunuch.

I did not tell Leonard about not bothering me about his other pet theory, the one where we used his public theory to transport someone backwards and forwards through time. I should have, but I doubt it would have made any difference. Finally after a week of this, I relented. I was just as excited and curious as he was.

"Tonight we go," I told Leonard. He was thrilled.

Leonard had managed, much to my surprise, to bring his contribution to this effort: money, namely old money. Leonard never trusted banks and much of his money was stashed in various places. I didn't know where, exactly, because he didn't have an apartment. But with his gift for breaking into rooms and appearing out of nowhere, I imagined thousands of dollars stashed in various pipes on the Columbia campus. The famous tunnels and pipes below campus could be stuffed with half a million dollars of Leonard's money. I managed to get some vintage clothes and we had no worries about Leonard, of course, Leonard always looked shabby.

We encoded the information to perform the quantum teleportation. I loaded it onto my hand-held. That was the only worry. I needed my computer and the apparatus to get back home. We packed the lasers in a suitcase, they were that small, and enough rolls of very thin metal to rig up a cage that was good enough, but I was worried I'd lose my Android computer. If this really worked, I was more nervous about what would happen if a 1950s person discovered my laptop. I figured at this stage we'd either be back in the fifties, dead, or sitting here staring at each other. I had briefly considered the fact that this laboratory didn't exist in 1958, the year we were shooting for, and that if this worked we might end up encased in schist, only to be discovered when the lab was built sometime in the eighties of whatever bubble we were going to go to.

"Have no fear young man. Let's go!"

I loaded the text file and pressed RUN on the program. Nothing happened. In my excitement, I mistyped the program name. Linux is unforgiving. Now I feared that there was a typo in the encoded numbers. They were only strings of numbers about two thousand pages long, but it had to encode precisely, correctly for the spooky action at a distance to work the way we wanted.

I typed the program again and waited. I wish I could say that there was a dramatic noise or flash or even a thud. There was none of that, no cloud. At once we were in the basement of my building and then we were in a basement somewhere else. Except that I knew, instantly, we were in the 1950s—quantum time travel worked.

All of a sudden I felt nauseous. Leonard looked around. For once he was quiet and he looked frightened even.

"Young man, I believe we've done it!"

"We have? Where are we? How do you even know?"

"I've been on this campus since 1951, don't you know. You think I don't know every room on this campus? You've heard the legends of the tunnels, I suppose? I know every single one." We sat in silence for about ten minutes until Leonard slapped me on the shoulder and said, "Come young man, let's explore."

We found ourselves in the basement of Fayerweather Hall. We walked out of Fayerweather onto the campus. Luckily it was an unusually warm November day. Both of us forgot winter coats. The campus seemed familiar, but also not. I cannot explain in enough detail how unsettling it was to walk out and see young people in garb that my parents would've worn. Nobody was talking on cellphones. A few young men were throwing footballs around, but there were no Frisbees. Most of the students were men. All the women technically went to Barnard. I saw almost no women in pants, most in long skirts holding their books in front of themselves, protectively. Almost all the women had makeup on. I was astonished.

"Leonard. We did it! We fucking did it!" I exclaimed and practically hugged him.

"Yes, we did." He had a faraway misty look in his eyes.

"Now, listen young man. You must remember you are in the fifties. People, especially people at an Ivy League university, didn't curse back then. You can't say *fuck*. Women were the fairer sex. Men held doors open for them, were chivalrous."

"Patronizing, you mean."

"If you say so, but remember, the world of the fifties is far different from our world of today. I remember it. Follow my lead. And try not to look so slack-jawed and astonished. Come, I'm hungry; I know a little luncheonette on Broadway that has the best egg creams. You can't even get them in the city anymore."

Leonard had to push me to walk towards Broadway. We passed a couple of laughing young men in crewcuts, then two women in long skirts, tight sweaters and push-up bras, giggling. Both wore pearls. I imagined they were flirting with the boys, but I didn't get how it was done. Then one of the girls lit a cigarette. I realized how many people were smoking, and also how almost all the people were white. Unlike the campus today.

Suddenly, Leonard stopped.

"Oh my God," he said.

"What is it?"

"Do you know who that is walking towards us?"

I saw a nondescript Asian man in a fifties style suit that hung loose on him, but he was wearing a very stylish tie with a hat. So many men wore hats.

"I have no idea."

"Tsung-Dao Lee. Everyone calls him T.D. He was a colleague of mine, I worked with him. He supported me during my, um, troubles. My God he looks so young."

"Leonard, remember what you told me. We're in another world, the T.D. you know or knew doesn't know you yet, does he?"

Lee came closer and stared at Leonard. He stopped and said with just a hint of a Chinese accent, "You're not Leonard Zavitsky's father are you?"

Leonard was stunned, I quickly stepped in.

"No, sir, we're just visiting the campus. This man is my grandfather and I am thinking of doing graduate studies here."

"Funny, you look so much like Leonard. Even have same mannerisms. Oh, well, perhaps it is better you are not related. The young man I refer to is a genius, but has no discipline. He will either be a Nobelist or a bum."

He began to walk away. Leonard looked thunderstruck by T.D.'s words. It was clear that he thought T.D. was a friend, a colleague, someone who believed in him.

"Oh, and young man," T.D. stopped and looked at me. "Columbia is a great institution. Good luck to you." And he walked off.

We continued walking slowly to Broadway. It was funny how the core campus looked the same as it should since most of the buildings were built before the fifties. Luckily Mudd hadn't been built yet. We walked past Alma Mater, past the Low Library steps where students were sitting. I was struck by how demurely they were sitting, all the women with their long skirts and their legs protectively crossed. Everyone was smoking.

Leonard stopped and we sat on a bench. Leonard held his head in his hands. I thought it was all too much for him. Here he was going back to when he was a young man, back to his beginnings.

"Leonard, what are you thinking?"

"Young man, I need a cigarette. I don't think I can take looking at the young me, at all these kids, some of whom I might know. Young man, I am a fraud, a cheat. I should have been stripped of my PhD. I am nothing but a failure."

"Leonard, come on. We're fu—I mean we're here because of you! Come on, let's walk around!"

"You go, you go on, I need to take care of something."

"Leonard, promise me you won't do anything rash. Remember, here you are in your twenties. The real you, the you that you are is pushing eighty. You have no past, not much money…"

"Paul, I know, but let me stay here. I need some time. I promise you we'll go back together. I need to do this."

I was not going to leave him and we sat for a bit. The more used to being on campus in the fifties I became, the more acclimated I was to the New York of the fifties, and the more I wanted to explore. Leonard was, surprisingly, becoming a drag.

I finally managed to march him to Broadway. Again I was stunned. I just stopped and stared at the cars and people walking up and down the streets. Everyone seemed so dressed up. Women pushed baby carriages in heels, skirts and hats. They pushed gigantic carriages too, not strollers. The air smelled different. The pollution was different. Then I remembered leaded gas. I silently hoped my few days' exposure wouldn't make me mad. Again I noticed how many people smoked and how few really fat people there were.

It began to cloud up and I had to drag Leonard to the luncheonette. I couldn't help noticing the magazines for sale. One magazine had a headline, "Will computers take over your job?" along with a picture of a huge old style ENIAC-like computer from the fifties. Well, this was the fifties. ENIAC was state-of-the-art. I took one look toward the street to see a passing bus. We sat down at two stools and I noticed the sugar dispensers in gleaming metal, also the ashtrays everywhere, and a mother admonishing a young boy for rotating around the stools. Leonard looked dazed. So did I, but for different reasons.

"Whadda you'll have?" said the woman behind the counter. She was dressed in a tight waitress uniform that reminded me of a nurse's uniform, but different. It was starched white. I stared at her and managed to stammer out, "Coffee for now, and do you have apple pie?"

"Wit or widdout?"

"Without please, and my friend will have an egg cream."

I turned to Leonard, barely able to contain my grin. "Leonard, snap out of it!"

I looked at the walls and noticed the signs for specials: Oxtail soup. Corned beef hash, open-faced turkey sandwich. Tuna salad, knockwurst, meatballs with spaghetti. Clam chowder. This was an old-time diner. I doubt they had ever heard of feta cheese, or turkey burgers. Two stools down I stared in wonder at a young, beautiful, mocha-skinned black woman. Like almost all women she was in a skirt. She also was wearing a white shirt and a beautiful multicoloured shawl. She was sipping a milkshake. Slowly sipping and then reading, as if considering every different taste of the milkshake. She was reading *Discourse on Colonialism* by Aimé Césaire. I had briefly dated a woman from Martinique in the nineties and to impress her I bought a copy and pretended to read it. I couldn't get through it. Politics wasn't something that I understood. I couldn't help but stare at this woman. She was beautiful, intellectual, and well, black, which meant that the neighbourhood wasn't totally different. She caught me staring and gave me a haughty look. I quickly looked away, embarrassed. She was probably a Barnard student. What was her life like? How did she manage to make it to Barnard in the fifties? Even in New York there was so much racism. How did she manage to cope? What was her life going to be? Would she be a pioneer or give up?

The place was beginning to fill with students. I wondered about all of them. How were their lives going to turn out? Who was going to get married, move to the suburbs and be boring? Who was going to die in Vietnam? Who was going to drop out and move to a commune in ten years' time? Were some of these students now professors or well-fed alumni in my Columbia? Were some of their names on plaques on the campus in my Columbia?

I tried to interest Leonard in this. "Hey, Leonard," I said, trying to fashion a more New York accent. "Who do you think the smart chicks are, who are the fast girls, the intellectuals?"

Leonard looked at me glumly and said, "You know, Paul, it really doesn't make a difference. I came to this world and I know, I know I will be a failure in this world. What we need to do is to go back further. I need to exorcise my ghosts and make me somebody in some quantum bubble. If there is only one quantum bubble where I know that Leonard Zavitsky didn't mess things up and throw away his life, I'll be satisfied.

I coughed because the smoke from the couple to Leonard's right was drifting towards us. I started to think of protesting when I realized everyone smoked and nobody thought about it. In this world, complaining about it would be seen as something only a selfish prig would do. As the male of the couple was large and well-muscled—I imagined him as what they would call a "letterman," perhaps on the football team or crew team—I judged that inadvisable. I just coughed a bit and sucked it up. I laughed to myself knowing that "suck it up" is a term that hadn't even been invented yet.

"Look, Leonard, let's assume you are the loser you are. There is one thing you did. You, and only you, provided the answer to make this, all of this happen! We're quantumnauts! Because of you Leonard." My coffee came and I held it up and said, "I salute you, Leonard Zavitsky." My apple pie came and I took a bite. I have to say it was the most delicious pie I had tasted in a long time. I realize that even in the fifties, the decade we think of as the beginning of TV dinners, most things were cooked from scratch. This pie had shortening, apples, probably lard, this pie was real!

Leonard sipped his egg cream and smiled slowly. "Yeah, I am a genius aren't I? You see this egg cream, young man? This we don't have back home anymore. This egg cream is real!" He held up his glass and we clinked. "To Quantumnauts!" he said, in the old New York accent where *–naut* sounds like *naught*.

"Leonard, what do we do now?" I asked after I finished my pie.

"Let's walk!"

We walked down Broadway. There were no new buildings, of course, and the Upper West Side looked far more middle-class than it does today. In some parts it was even shabby. I kept up a non-stop narrative of the cars, noticing how huge they were, how they were all American, how curved they were. I saw two-toned cars with huge tail fins. They looked so ordinary and in place here. I noticed the children, unaccompanied and just out playing children's games, hopscotch, stickball, no parents hovering over them.

Finally, after we got to about 72nd street I asked Leonard, "Where are we walking?"

He said, "Young man, don't fret, but I need a moment to myself. Can you meet me later tonight, at this address?" I wrote it down: 128 West 61st street. "You can take the subway or the EL. We have them here."

"But Leonard, will you be all right?"

"I assure you, young man; I will not do anything to embarrass you. I did have a life you know. I need to know it again, to see it again. Now go! And don't think of following me."

As much as I wanted to follow him I didn't. Perhaps he had a girl. Perhaps a boyfriend, I will never know. I wanted to keep that aspect of Leonard secret. We had shared so many intimacies, but this, well there still had to be some secrets.

I was tired of walking but wanted to go back to campus. I walked to the 72nd street IRT stop. I realized I had no idea how to actually use the subway of the fifties. Did you buy tokens?

Did you use coins? I was a tourist in my own city. It was an exhilarating and also scary feeling. I quickly figured out how to buy a token and put it in the turnstile. An old unshaven man in a shabby coat was slowly walking and half falling down the stairs. He looked familiar. It looked like Red. I ran to him and tapped him on the shoulder.

"Red!" I exclaimed.

Well it looked like Red but it wasn't and he gave me a glare of utter hostility.

"I ain't who you think I am son, and you best leave me be."

"Sorry," I stammered. Was this the hint of quantum strangeness that Leonard talked about? Was this Red, only a Red who couldn't go home again, and was driven crazy by it?

The car came with a very loud clackety whoosh. I hadn't realized how quiet modern subway cars were compared to those in the fifties. The subway was ear-splitting. I took the IRT north to Columbia. I noticed the ads. Cigarettes, whisky, and one for a holiday in Cuba, which I thought funny. The airline promised quiet, safe, smooth flights on their DC-7 propliners. A drawing of a couple wearing straw hats, drinks in hand, smiled at the train passengers.

I got off the train and walked to campus. I wanted to go to Mudd to see what would be my office, but of course it isn't my office, and Mudd wouldn't be built for another ten years or so. My office doesn't exist yet. I decided to sit on the stairs in front of the library soaking up the campus. Two women sat near me, one a slightly heavy-set young lady wearing jeans and a sweater. She was the only female student I had seen wearing jeans. The cuffs were turned up almost four inches yet she had on saddle shoes.

Her hair was dark and in a bun. Although heavy-set she was curvy and had a serious air about her. Next to her, taking a drag on her cigarette, was a beautiful redhead wearing a tight cream-coloured dress with a green belt. She had on bright red lipstick and had her hair held up by a barrette. They were both holding books and I tried to be as discreet as possible in looking at the titles, but I wasn't successful. I heard snatches of conversation.

"Elise, I don't want to tell you what to do, but he is simply a dreamboat," the brunette said to the redhead.

"Yeah, I know, but he is an idiot." They both giggled.

"Aren't all men idiots?"

"Yeah, but I mean, he treats me like I am some girl from Long Island come to Barnard for a husband."

"Well, half the time I think that's what most of us girls are here for?" More giggles.

"Yeah, but I have had my eyes opened. Here in the city there's art, there's life, there's…"

"Boys! Negroes."

"Yes, I slept with him, do you think me cheap?" The redhead looked away, but also wore a slight smile.

"You slept with Claude? You're kidding me. No! But if anyone found out?"

"Nobody ever will, we're not stupid. He lived in the south for a while, you know, and he tells me that things aren't that great for negroes in New York either. He says at least in the south he knew everyone hated him just because he was black. But anyway, he doesn't want to get lynched. Anyway, I thought I loved him but I don't. You won't tell anyone. I think I have sort of a reputation."

"El, what sort of reputation do you want?"

"Smart!" the beautiful Elise said. "Josie, can I share a secret with you?"

"Go ahead, you share everything with me."

"Claude and I, well, I smoked marijuana once with him."

The brunette looked shocked, and then concerned.

"You're kidding, Elise, I don't know, is he trying to hook you into anything?"

"No, no. I don't even see him anymore. Plus, your beatnik friends probably smoke it too."

"El, how do you know what my friends do? You always look down on them."

"No I don't."

"Yes you do. You're always making fun of them, calling them hairy and smelly."

Elise began to protest but Josie cut her off.

"You know, you talk a good game, but this campus isn't where it's at. It's just a training ground for bankers and lawyers, and us—future housewives. Come on down to the village tonight. John Coltrane is going to play."

"No, I can't abide jazz."

"It's the music of the oppressed. Look, we can't understand because we're not oppressed. Have you ever read *Tristes Tropiques*?"

"No, Josie, look. Just because I don't like jazz doesn't make me a square. We are oppressed. We women. Our lives are programmed to be good girls, never to have any," and here she whispered something.

Josie looked shocked and she looked around. She saw me and I did my best to act as if I was ignoring them.

Josie said, "Elise, I don't want to be stuck in the suburbs with three kids, a Studebaker and frozen peas either, and I don't even care if you are fast, but well, if you use your sex appeal then you are just like what they want you to be. A piece of meat."

They both took long drags on their cigarettes. Elise spoke. "Josie, wouldn't it be great to go to Europe? We could do Italy, France, oh the dreamy French guys, we'd paint at the Boulevard Saint-Germain, eat baguettes, forget this plastic world."

"We wouldn't bathe!"

"We wouldn't shave!"

They both laughed.

"So El, what are you going to do about Joseph? Are you, you know, serious?"

"If you want to know my sex life, the answer is no. Claude was a one-time special thing, a special fling. He is as close to French as I will ever get. No, with Joseph I am a good girl. That is what is programmed for us isn't it Josie."

Josie and Elise sat for a few minutes and Elise got a very faraway look.

"Frankly, Joseph bores the shit out of me, Josie. I can't take it any more."

"Why?"

"He never listens to a thing I say, he always tells me how pretty I am."

"But you are, all the boys notice you, they never notice me."

"But this is what you just finished telling me. We're more than pretty faces, you know. I want someone, some man, to look at me and care what the hell I think. I want them to actually listen to what I say."

"Men never care what we think. They are only out for one thing. You are beautiful, *ergo*, you have power. The only power we women have."

"Well, Josie, maybe it's power to make life, power to control men. Our women power makes men afraid."

"Elise, you have the power, I don't. Nobody even looks at me."

Josie stopped suddenly and asked Elise, "Have you ever read *Herland*?"

"No, what is it?"

Josie described the feminist paradise that existed, until men came to fuck it up. I remember being forced to read it in a freshman class and found it dated, and a bit ridiculous.

"Sounds lesbian," Elise said.

"Oh, be serious! You talk about how men only look at you as a piece of meat; well, we have to fight to be recognized. Just like the Puerto Ricans, just like the Negroes."

Now Elise is surprised. I stifle a chuckle, barely hiding the fact that I am listening in.

"Well, I will strike the first symbolic blow for women. I am dumping Joseph and that idiot crewcut of his. I'll never have to read up on what the Yankees are doing, or what Y.A. Tittle is doing."

They both laughed. Just then Josie spied me.

"You there, man." Both Josie and Elise laughed.

"What are the Yankees doing today?"

"I have no idea," I replied. "I suppose out sailing their clippers or eating chowder."

They both laughed. Elise said, "Well, Josie, we have a man with a sense of humour."

She turned to me, "Elise Fein, and this is my friend Josephine Buxbaum, Josie for short."

"How do you do," I stammered.

Josie looked at me, "You weren't listening to us, were you? It is all girl talk, scintillating girl talk."

"Not listening at all, just enjoying the sun. It is a beautiful day, isn't it? Gorgeous for November."

"Say, you don't have any books, you don't have a briefcase. Are you a student here? A prof?"

"Well," I began to say and then stopped. How can I tell these two women that I am a post doc and a grad student here, only sixty years later in time. I had to think of something fast. Real fast.

Elise turned to Josie and stage whispered, "Well, I think the cat's got this boy's tongue, I do." Elise said this in a mock flirtatious southern accent.

"Well, I'm a visiting scholar, in the physics department. Just finding my way around campus."

"Visiting, from where?" Josie asked.

"Stanford, out in California," I stammered, hoping that she didn't have a brother who went there.

"Wow that must be great, sunny weather all day, palm trees."

"Well, actually, it gets kinda rainy in the winter, and you've got those earthquakes."

I've been to Stanford and figure I know enough about it to bluff my way through. I just hope I don't say anything that will give away the fact that I am from the future—flub the name of a president or a senator, or divulge the outcome of a historical event that is still happening. Yet, still, I am flirting with these women. It seems so easy to talk to them. They seem so bold and forward for these times, yet they want to be bold and forward with me. Perhaps they view me as harmless, that's why.

Josie piped up.

"Physics. Frankly, I see it as the science that gave us the H-bomb. But, you don't seem like the type to do that kind of research, do you?" She arched an eyebrow like a school marm.

"Well?"

"What research do you do?" asked Elise.

"Well, it's sort of complicated and hard to say."

"Flashes of anger," Elise says in a quiet voice. "Yeah, I know, we're girls. Fun to discuss literature, maybe philosophy, maybe shock us with some crap in *Playboy*, but the hard stuff, no we wouldn't understand because we're girls."

"Actually, you wouldn't understand because, well, I don't even understand it. Look, I am sorry; I didn't mean to be condescending. I'm not too good at expressing myself." The old embarrassment takes hold.

"I can see that." Josie said, laughing.

"Leave the boy alone," said Elise, "can't you see he is tongue-tied."

"OK Mr., try us, what sort of physics do you do? Are you going to burn the Russkies, the Red Chinese? We're modern girls, we can take it. Oh, by the way, we don't even know your name?"

"Pavel, Pavel Feldman, but everyone calls me Paul."

"Pavel, isn't that Russian?"

"Yeah, well my parents were Reds, um, back in the thirties and they gave me the name, but please call me Paul."

"Well," Josie said, "you better explain physics to us quick, I have a class."

"I'm skipping my class today. The professor has bad breath and Joseph will be there. I can't see him, he'll be all over me."

Josie walked off. I got the impression that she regarded me as some lesser sort, some kind of man who melds into the woodwork. She scarcely said goodbye to me.

Elise took out another cigarette and put it in her mouth. She waited. Finally she sighed and took out a match and lit the cigarette. Almost distractedly she offered me one.

"No thanks, I don't smoke. So what is the class?"

"You don't smoke, why?"

"Never developed the habit, it seems silly to inhale burning stuff into your lungs. And the lung cancer…" I stop. When the hell did the surgeon general's report come out anyway?

"I've heard of that but I don't believe it, plus a girl has got to keep her figure!" Elise jokes.

An awkward silence spreads between us, so I ask again, "What's the class that you're skipping?"

She laughed.

"Well, actually, it is introduction to physics for non-scientists. I am the only girl in the class. I only took it so I could take notes for Joseph, my boyfriend. I mean, ex-boyfriend. Do you know Leonard Zavitsky?"

My mouth dropped to the floor. I started to laugh, laugh hard.

"Don't tell me he is your instructor?"

"Yeah, do you know him? Can I ask you why he stinks? Does he ever take a bath?"

"Well, he is one of the most brilliant persons I know, but yeah, he is not much in the hygiene department."

"How does his wife deal with that?"

"Well, I don't know if he has a wife."

"Is he a queer? I mean, I don't care if he is. I think Josie might be."

"No I think he is truly asexual. He lives only for math and physics. So what is good old Leonard teaching you?"

I inched my way towards her and we talked for the better part of an hour. We moved from the stairs to the lawn where I chivalrously took off my jacket and she lay on it, so as to not muss her skirt.

We talked about mathematics, about Leonard. She could not abide him—thought he was pretentious, but I told her that was just Leonard and not to take it personally. She told me about Joseph, who was her football-playing soon-to-be ex-boyfriend. She admitted she was a tease, and was interested in him at first.

"He is a dreamboat and a good catch" was her phrase, but "God does he bore me. I am just a trinket to him. He actually calls me 'my trinket.'"

Elise stopped suddenly and said to me, "You know, if I was a man, I think I could really be a scientist, you know? Have you ever heard of Heisenberg's uncertainty principle?"

"Well, um, yeah. I do work in the physics department after all."

"So you know how strange the quantum world is. But nobody knows it. Think of the possibilities. Have you ever heard of quantum entanglement? This Zavitsky is teaching an intro to physics course for non-scientists—the one I'm taking—and he keeps on ranting about quantum entanglement. Nobody understands him. But the thing is, Paul, I do. I hate the man but I get it. I don't get the math entirely, not because I am a girl, but because I am not a math genius, but I get the, oh, the gestalt of it, you know how they call it a *Gedankenexperiment*? Well, if you *gedank* you realize that nothing you perceive as real is real. We are all simply wave functions. Perhaps all we were were thoughts, distortions of energy?"

And for two more hours, until the sun went down and it grew colder, we talked and we talked—about physics, reality, philosophy, and feminism. Elise was much smarter than she appeared, but if I had my eyes open most people probably were.

Finally at about four-thirty she said, "Look, I've got to go. It was great talking to you, maybe I'll see you around."

Awkwardness. She will not be seeing me around, or if she did it will be a half-century in the future and she'll be showing her surly, pierced, tattooed grandchildren around Columbia's campus.

"Well, yeah Elise, it was really great talking to you. Perhaps, I don't know, perhaps we can catch some dinner."

She looked at me and said, "No, I have to break up with my boyfriend. But if you want, meet me at Lewisohn Stadium tonight at eight sharp. I have two tickets to a concert and, well, he wouldn't want to go anyway. Bye."

She gave me a coquettish wave and was off. I was sure she was swaying more than was necessary. Lewisohn Stadium! I had never even heard of it. And I had to meet Leonard now. I did something I don't ever do in modern New York. I hailed a cab. It was a large checker cab, huge really. I gave the driver the address and tried to strike up a conversation.

"Boy, they really make these cabs large nowadays."

"Huh? It's a cab, same as it's always been," said the driver.

He was not the talkative garrulous old-time New York cabbie. He looked like he'd had his nose broken in three places and he looked like he broke quite a few noses on other people. Soon I was at the address that was given. I tipped him well but he simply shrugged. The address Leonard gave me was of a nondescript brownstone on a nondescript block. I realized that the block was nothing but highrises nowadays.

I recognized Leonard walking towards me.

"Young man, young man, my work is almost done."

"Leonard, good to see you. Isn't this great!" I waved my hand all around the block. I noticed Leonard was smiling, beaming actually.

"Leonard, you look so happy, I've never seen you like this."

"Young man, we need to stay here a few days. I've secured quarters. Come."

The neighbourhood was where Lincoln Center is today, but in those days it was more of a slum. The old New York suspicion welled into me as I saw teenagers smoking, smirking and walking with swagger. Metal garbage cans, "ash cans" they called them in those days, were filled to overflowing. Next to an early fifties model car, a black man wearing a suit, white hat and loud tie was smoking a cigar. Leonard walked up to him and said, "It's good to see you. It's been a long time." I did not like this. Leonard forgets that the Leonard people knew was Leonard as a young man.

"Who the fuck are you old man?"

"Ah, Ronald, let's just say I am an older relative of a young man you know. Leonard. My young friend and I need lodgings for the night."

"You Leonard's grandpa or something. He is one crazy cat."

"Not exactly his grandpa, and please tell Maria Leonard is sorry."

"Yeah, lotta men fall in love with Maria, but only Leonard wants to save her. She don't wanna be saved though, you know. It ain't her time to be saved."

"Ah, young man, as always you are so right, so can you secure us quarters?"

"You never heard of a hotel?"

"Too many questions would be asked. Let's just say we're on a secret mission. Would this help us secure lodgings?"

From Leonard's pocket he took out a five hundred-dollar bill. I had forgotten that there used to be such large bills.

Ronald's eyes widened as he took it and then Leonard pushed another five hundred and said, "Please give Leonard this message, 'A circle, not a line,' he'll know what it means, and please, whatever you do, don't tell him, Maria, or anyone that you saw us."

Ronald asked, "Now what kind of trouble are you in and are you guys queer, coz I am running a respectable joint. Lot of white cats come for Puerto Rican or Negro tail and I am down with that, we are all brothers, your young friend Leonard even knows John Coltrane, like on a first name basis, but I will not have queers in my home."

"I assure you we are not, he is not. I am too old for anything."

"Want any weed?"

"Certainly not, Ronald."

"Um, I'd like some," I piped up rather surprising myself.

Leonard looked at me and scrunched up his eyes. "Young man, do you know what you are doing? In the fifties you could go to jail for a long time for possession."

"I know, Leonard. But, well, I met a gal. As long as we're here, well I want to impress her and show her what a hip cat I am."

Ronald looked at me and said, "Son, in this world, the next world, or any world you will never be a hip cat. Some men are, most men aren't. They just blend into the background. Probably better that way, take it from me."

I started to protest. I thought I'd even get angry and show what a man I am but Leonard stopped me.

"All right, Ronald, get my young swain some locoweed, and also Ronald, your son?"

All of a sudden Ronald glared at him suspiciously, remembered his cigar ash and shook off the end perilously close to Leonard's shoes. Leonard didn't notice.

"Ronald, your son will grow up to be a brilliant man, a scientist, a man who will change the world. Trust me. Trust Maria." Leonard looked into Ronald's eyes in a commanding, piercing way, such that I had never seen. Ronald just looked wide-eyed.

"Trust me, Ronald, he will change the world if you let him."

Ronald smiled, and held out his hand. Leonard shook it and Ronald said, "OK, old man, you got a room, I presume you know where."

"Two beds, please," I piped up.

Leonard said, "Two rooms, maybe my young friend will get lucky."

"I doubt it," said Ronald and walked away.

We began to walk toward Central park and two teenagers came walking towards us. The boy was skinny, with reddish blond hair in a greaser ducktail, wearing blue jeans with cuffs turned up about five inches and boots that looked sort of like Doc Martens, but not exactly. It surprised me that kids wore boots like that in the fifties. The girl was a beautiful mocha-coloured teen with long black hair, a blue sweater and a long skirt, and sneakers. She was chewing gum. They stared at us and walked right into us, jostling Leonard hard. The boy said, "Go back to Brooklyn you sheeny motherfuckers," and they both laughed.

I started to get angry but Leonard stopped me. "Young man, this isn't your world, you don't want to start anything in this neighbourhood. You must trust me on this. You ever see *West Side Story?*"

"Yeah, they sang and danced a lot," I said with what I thought was biting wit.

"No, young man, that's not what I mean. New York in these times is tribal. Manhattan was filled with neighbourhoods, the blacks the whites, the Italians, Jews, Irish, Puerto Ricans, they all had their own turf and woe betide anyone who walked on another's turf. Gentrification, that word hasn't even been invented. You must remember that, Paul, keep your emotions in check. Consider this an anthropological expedition."

We walked further on 61st Street and we passed young boys playing stickball and people hanging out and talking on stoops, enjoying the unseasonably warm day. They simply no longer do this in Manhattan.

"So are you going to tell me," I asked.

"Tell you what, young man?"

I grinned and asked, "Who the fuck are Maria and Ronald?"

"It's not what you think."

We walked on in silence, finally he said, "In these times, men went to whores. Single men, I mean. Women didn't spread their legs and put out at the first sign of romance, you know."

"You put it so delicately, I am sure no woman can resist your charms."

"Young man, you should know by now my personal habits are not some mere idiosyncrasies. I abhor sex and sexual contact. You know Erdős, right?"

"Well, not personally. I am sure my Erdős' number is in the triple digits."

"Stick with me, young man, and you'll get an Erdős of two. But Erdős, he was such a genius, he lived only for math. He would wander around like a vagabond. He lived life on an elegiac plain. You see true intellect requires little."

I cut him off and I said smiling, trying my best fifties detective novel, "Who are Ronald and Maria."

"Well, Maria was a lady of the evening and Ron was her procurer. Of course, single colleagues, even in universities, would try to prove their manhood by having a drunken night on the town. Well, as asexual as I was, I knew I couldn't refuse. Otherwise I would be thought queer. You know, there was no gay liberation or rights in this era, son. If someone thought you engaged in Spartan love, your career, maybe your life, would be over. At the very least you'd be forced to see a psychiatrist."

"I watch the History channel you know, stop changing the subject."

"I don't have a TV. You mean to say in our future there is an entire channel devoted to history?"

I couldn't tell if he was trying to be funny or not.

"Leonard, stop changing the freakin' subject."

"OK, well, so I picked Maria, and well she had a son. A prodigy, young man, a prodigy. Maria and I never did it but I paid her well. I would rest for an hour and read, or read to her son. I would show him math problems and he just sat there wide-eyed and drank it all in. As long as Maria got paid, she didn't care. Do you know her son was Ronald's boy?"

"I gathered that."

"Well, what do you think the chances were for a half-black half-Puerto Rican math genius in this area in this time period? None! I tell you, none. So I said to myself, my younger self, 'You have got to save this boy.' And I tried, I really tried, but the more I read to the boy, the more I saw Maria, the more jealous Ron got. It was strange, when he thought I was shtupping his girl for money, he didn't care, but when he thought his girl and I formed a bond, he got crazy."

"So, what happened to the boy?"

"In our world, I don't know, but it has always kind of haunted me. He could've been someone, he could've been the next Einstein with the right mentorship, but well, in our world, I just have no idea. In our world, Ronald made it plain that no pansy-ass like me was gonna come between him and his kid."

"Touching," I said with a bit of sarcasm.

As we walked toward Central Park, rather aimlessly, I remembered my date with Elise. I suddenly told Leonard that I had to go. He looked at me and smiled, "You won't get laid young man, trust me, only whores give it away without a ring. And remember our pact, non-interference, we are anthropologists."

"The prime directive, I know."

He didn't get that. I doubt he knew anything about popular culture, or really high culture. I grabbed a cab, again marvelling at the huge size of it, and told the driver, "Lewisohn Stadium." I realized I had no idea where it was, it could have been in New Jersey for all I knew.

We drove uptown. I noticed that the cab driver was a woman with an Italian accent. She wasn't talkative either, except for the string of curses she would spew out at traffic. We took Central Park West uptown and I was struck by how much darker Manhattan was. There was so much neon on Broadway but the apartments, traffic, and street lights simply did not give off the glow that modern lights do. The light that it did give off infused the streetscape with a yellowish air of coldness. I felt like I was on some film noir stage set. At 125th Street we turned onto Broadway. We passed low-rise tenements that I knew in my day would be high-rise housing. We turned north on Broadway and where there are now self-storage warehouses stood factories, tenements and grocery stores. We finally made it to Lewisohn Stadium. I had no idea such a place existed in New York. It looked like some sort of Greek amphitheatre. I imagined ancient playwrights staging their plays here. I was struck by how white the columns were, and by how white the people were. In my New York this neighbourhood is almost all Dominican. I doubted I could find a Presidente beer at the local bar in this time.

I realized I had no way of finding Elise and I wondered if this was just her way to blow me off. I began to look at the crowd of mostly middle-aged people when I felt a tap at my back. It was Elise. She gave me a quick smile, and I stood astonished. I hadn't changed, what would I change into? But she was resplendent in her long skirt, pearls and a checked coat. She smiled, laughed and put her hand out. "Paul, Pavel, I am so glad you could make it."

"I wouldn't miss it for the world, thank you for inviting me." I had to ask, "So what happened with…"

"Well, he didn't take it so well, called me a punk, a cocktease."

"That's awful language."

"Well, from his perspective, I guess I was. On paper he is everything my folks would want, what any girl would want, you know?"

"I have no idea what a girl would want." I tried to arch my eyes like I was being world-weary. I felt stupendously foolish saying this.

"No man does, maybe no girl does. But you know we just want to be, well, we have brains, you know? Not just bodies ready to birth and then to keep the house tidy."

I smiled and said, "Well, how much do I owe you for the tickets?"

She frowned and said, "Why Pavel—do you mind if I call you Pavel, it sounds so exotic—that's insulting. It's on me. Joseph got them so I am going to use them. I hope you like Pete Seeger, have you heard of him?"

I struggled not to guffaw. How can I tell her that in my

world Pete Seeger was a man who lived to his nineties and gave himself to a lot of lefty liberal causes but is someone for my grandfather's time.

"I love him," I say enthusiastically, perhaps a little too loud. I mentally struggled to remember any songs my parents might have listened to. I do remember hearing him play the banjo on a sailing ship that travels up the Hudson to draw attention to pollution. I don't think pollution is an issue yet in this world.

"Good." She takes my hand and runs towards the entrance. "Keep up, Pavel, keep up!"

The crowd was light, for it was November and usually concerts stopped at the end of summer but this was a special autumn concert, and, well, it was a nice night.

By now I was hopelessly infatuated with Elise. She was young, she was beautiful, she was smart, and she oozed a sort of sensuality. I wasn't prepared for that from women in that era. The times being what they were, her sex appeal was probably the only thing she could use to stand out, to be recognized. She knew how to use it very well and she was using it on me! Yet she also knew her brains would go to waste. I sensed that when she wasn't "on" in unguarded moments she looked down and her beautiful smile turned into a grimace. Unless she was either very rich, very independent, or very special, the life curve for Elise was set: marry a doctor, have a few kids, maybe be a teacher or a school administrator and then take ceramics classes when older or until women's lib hit. I was beginning to realize that the realness of past times I glimpsed in old photographs masked a crushing veil of conflicting and competing expectations. Nobody was free here.

The concert was uninspiring. It was hard to reconcile the young Seeger with the old man singing tired protest songs that I knew. I was secretly praying that Seeger wouldn't launch into "Kumbaya."

We got through the evening without a "Kumbaya," and now my shyness and cluelessness around women showed its face. Do I invite her for a late bite to eat? Where? I have no idea about anything in this New York, I am as much a tourist as some hayseed off the train from Kansas.

We exited the stadium slowly, neither of us saying much. I felt awkward. Finally I said, "Man, I'm hungry, do you want to go for a bite to eat?"

Luckily she smiled a bit and said, "Yeah, but there's nothing up here. I know a place near campus, but it's well, it's Indian. Are you familiar with Indian food? No cows."

She flashed a dazzling smile at me.

"I'm a vegetarian, I love Indian food!"

I was generally surprised that there were any "ethnic" restaurants in New York in the fifties, but I shouldn't have been. It was New York after all, if there were going to be any East Indians in the U.S. in 1958, it was going to be in New York.

The restaurant was on 120th street and we decided to walk down Broadway. The noise of the train was familiar, but I still couldn't help but notice the small soda fountains, butcher shops, and the like.

"Pavel, you seem like a tourist, like you've never been to New York ever before."

This was dangerous territory. I was born in Long Island, like Elise, but her Long Island and mine were two different worlds.

"Well I was born in Long Island, but we moved a lot. My parents, my dad, had a hunch to live off the land so we moved to the Hudson Valley."

"You mean like, what? Poughkeepsie or something? That sounds so square, if you don't mind my saying."

"Well, it was typical, you might say."

"Any brothers and sisters?"

"Nope, I am an only child," I lied. The concepts of the half-sister and two half-brothers from my parents' other marriages would have been far too complicated to explain. I began to realize that almost anything would be complicated.

"What about you Elise? I know you're from Long Island."

"Well, born in Brooklyn, go Dodgers! But we moved out to Oceanside when my dad got home from the war."

"Must have been tough not to see your father during the war."

"Yeah, but that was for everyone. What did your dad do in the war?"

"Well, not much." I couldn't think fast enough. I was beginning to be ashamed about my misleading Elise, I had no right to do this. She sensed the diffidence, but not the reason behind it.

She touched my arm as we made it to the restaurant and said, "Don't worry. Lots of people were scared. I'd be. And the men who came back. Never the same."

"Thanks."

"You know, Pavel, I talk about how women have a raw deal but in some ways men have it tougher. They have to fight. Whether they want to or not. You know, Joseph, well he really has a soft side, you wouldn't notice it, but he can't show it. The world would eat him up. You men don't have any more choice than we do. My dad is a cream puff but nobody knows that. The only time I saw him cry was when the Dodgers moved to California."

Silence as we sat down and the waiter came over. He was dressed up in stage Indian garb and an exaggerated turban. He bowed and handed us menus addressing us as "Sahib" and "Memsahib." Indian music played in the background, yet the staff, the décor, seemed absurd.

"Gee, I don't know what to order; frankly, some of this stuff is so strange."

"Elise, allow me. I am a bit of a connoisseur."

I ordered for the both of us, some chicken tikka masala without the chicken for me but with vegetables. The waiter assured me the chef would be delighted to make it more traditional. I asked for lentil *daal* which they usually had off-label only for diplomats from home. I also asked for pappadum and if they could make a *lassi*.

"No, sahib, I am afraid we cannot get mangoes in New York."

"No, I didn't think so. Oh well."

Elise looked at me kind of strange. "How do you know so much about Indian food? And what the heck is a *lassi* anyway?"

"Well, it's a long story."

"I've got all night," Elise looked at me and batted her eyes, her leg gently brushing up against my legs. She put her head in her hands and stared at me. "Well, Mr. Lassie, come home?"

"Well, I was in India, about seven years ago." That part was technically true. I was in India, but of course I was doing coursework with some legendary Indian physicists and computer engineers. But it was close enough. I just had to remember that Goa was still part of Portugal in this bubble.

"Really, how old were you then? I mean how old are you now?"

"Thirty." I made a mental calculation about what I was supposed to have seen or been. I thought luckily there was no war but there was one.

"Was this an army post?"

"Well, as a matter of fact it was. You see, it was during the Korean War, and India was newly independent, and well I was a math prodigy, or at least people thought I was a prodigy."

"Modest."

"Well, they knew I wouldn't make much of a soldier but they thought if they sent pencilnecks like me to India to help train Indian scientists, groom them, we could be allies."

"Wouldn't it make sense to bring them here?"

"Well, we wanted to give them the technology so they could develop and not go communist."

"Frankly, it seems with all the poverty there, the last thing they need is a bunch of kids fresh out of school bossing them around. I hope you don't mind my frankness."

"On the contrary, *it is* refreshing."

"Most men, most people actually, hate honesty. You want something else that's honest?"

"I'm not sure."

"Well *that's* honest. But, well, sometimes I feel you are not who you are, like you're hiding something, almost like you are a spy. Am I prying?"

"Well, I have a lot of baggage in my past, let's just say that."

She dropped it once the food came. The food was far more bland than the food that I know in my New York, but was spicy enough for Elise. Most of the rest of the dinner was passed with polite small talk. Elise was twenty-one, in her third year at Barnard with a major in anthropology. She held out Claude Lévi-Strauss as a hero. She was not looking forward to graduating because being a career gal meant a secretary, school teacher, or something similar. Her dreams were to go to Paris, or Latin America, anywhere where she could be something other than a Jewish housewife from Long Island.

"So do it, Elise! You can, you know."

"I love your enthusiasm, young man, but..."

Here I had to stifle a smile as I lit a cigarette for Elise.

"What's so funny?"

"Nothing, just an old friend of mine, sort of a physics mentor, he calls me 'young man', never—well, almost never—by my name."

"That is so queer. You know the instructor you know, who teaches my physics class, he does that to all the boys, drives Joseph wild. I wouldn't be surprised if Joseph got up one day and hit him. Of course that would be pure Joseph. Sorry, I am not supposed to talk about ex-boyfriends to men. It turns them off."

I felt Elise's leg against mine again. I was no longer interested in my food, which was no good by standards of my New York. I was infatuated with Elise, completely besotted. I also knew that she liked me. I had no idea what to do with this knowledge. Fortunately, Elise made it easy.

"Walk me home?"

"Sure, where's home?"

"I actually don't live on campus, my folks rent me an apartment. They actually think it's better for me, that I'd be less tempted by, I don't know what, lesbianism or moral corruption by boys."

We talked an easy talk on the way to her apartment. When we got there it was already late, she reminded me. We were at her front door. I noticed metal garbage cans, ash cans, to the left side of the door. I also saw a lack of Chinese food menus, or electronic buzzers near the front door. For a minute I wondered how people in apartments without doormen managed to be let in. I was about to lean in for a kiss when I heard an ungodly hiss and roar.

"Oh God, Goldie!" It was a feral cat that emerged from behind the ash can, with yellow fur and one eye. The cat had taken a shine to Elise.

"Sorry, Goldie, no tuna fish now, but I'll come down and bring you some soon."

"You a cat lover?"

"Yeah, I'm a cat cat," she said. It took me a while to recognize the pun. "I'd take her in, honestly, but my roommate is allergic. Well, I had a nice time."

Visions of my fifties ladies' man career already in my mental rear-view mirror, I awkwardly kissed her on the cheek and smiled. I managed to stammer out, "Can I see you soon?"

"I thought you'd never ask young, shy Pavel, how long are you in town for?"

"Well, a few days at least," and I added, "perhaps my gig might be a permanent one."

"Well then."

"Well," I finally stammered. "How about tomorrow night, if it isn't too much notice, I mean, um, well we can catch some music downtown."

"Well, yes we can as a matter of fact. Do you know how to reach me?"

She gave me her number, and then put her hand out. We shook hands and we kissed again, a bit more passionately this time. She turned and stage whispered, "Good night."

AND QUANTA CREATED WOMAN

I walked all the way down to 61st Street, a feat for which Leonard admonished me, but the neighbourhood seemed safe once I knew to dodge the teenagers. Most of the stores were closed or closing. It seemed with each block I walked the flashing neon signs, flashed off one last time in unison. Automobile traffic became surprisingly scanty and there wasn't a cab about. On 61st Street as I walked to the slightly less dingy brownstown where Leonard and I were staying, a policeman on the beat twirling his billy club walked along the curb towards me. I nodded a quick 'evening officer,' and he smiled at me and gave a harrumph. To him, just a client, probably a dentist from Queens. He'll get his cut in the morning.

When I told Leonard about Elise he was surprisingly upset.

"Young man, you know we are not supposed to be interfering, we are not of this world. You'll see her tomorrow night, get a quick kiss and break her heart. You know we're leaving to go back home the day after."

"You, Leonard, you are trying to save some kid you didn't save because of why, I have no idea. You realize that even if you do whatever heroism you think you're doing, the kid might still be an unknown no-account in this bubble's twenty-first century? You realize that once we traverse this bubble all bets are off."

"Paul, young man, do not remind me of what I invented. I know that, I know of the infinitudes of possibilities. I come here not for a second chance, nor even to effect change, but to exorcise my personal ghosts. You wouldn't understand."

"No, I am not Erdős, but you know, maybe I am doing a little personal ghost exorcising myself, you know? Fuck!"

With that I tried to go to sleep. But I asked, "Leonard, I need practical advice. I'm taking Elise out, and I need threads, new clothes, what does a young hipcat wear nowadays?"

"Young man, you should know by now that asking me that is like asking me for sex advice. I have no idea. Ask Ronald."

"Ok, well do you know where I should go, where I should take her?"

"Oh, that I do young man, go to the village, take her to a beatnik café, maybe even a jazz bar, you will be in her knickers by nightfall, if that is what you want."

"Leonard, I'm not that kind of man." Leonard laughed at that. A few minutes later, I realized. "Leonard, I don't have any money left, I mean fifties money. May I . . ."

"Borrow some? Of course, I feel like your father. But under one condition."

"Name it."

"You get protection. Go to a drugstore and get some prophylactics. You know, rubbers."

"Oh jeez, Leonard."

After a few minutes of silence, I turned to him. "Leonard, thanks. I mean, really, thanks."

The next day Leonard and I got up. I saw Ronald, but still no Maria or the boy whose name I still didn't know. Whereas the autumn in New York lived up to its name yesterday, today was dreary and drizzly, with the leaves on all the street trees, including the beautiful yellow honey locusts now on the sidewalk like so many bits of sticky sallow confetti. The party was over.

Still, Leonard was in fine form. He and I walked to a coffee shop where he ordered eggs, home fries and coffee. He bought a newspaper and a cigar at the luncheonette across the street and read it and puffed the cigar while I tried to eat my eggs, no sausage, no bacon for me yet.

"Listen to this, young man. They're calling it the most amazing technological breakthrough of the year."

"I know, Leonard, but you know how that worked out."

"Yes, but you and I know how it should've worked out..." A waitress filled our coffees and left, addressing me as "Hon." I stifled an urge to call her "sugar." I was still a tyro in this world.

Leonard, however, was not shy, "Thank you my dear child," he said. And then he said, "Please tell the proprietor that the Chicago Cardinals will cream the Giants. He doesn't know me but I know him. Please tell him."

Leonard turned to me, "A good turn for a good man with a bad habit."

"I never knew you were a sports fan."

"I am not. I'm just a math man, the numbers and statistics of sports are fascinating. You know, young man, for a while I even thought there was some hidden order, a sort of statistical steganography that only I can reveal."

"Is there?"

"Yes, young man, but it isn't in which quarterman throws the longest touchdown yard. We know what it is don't we." He uncharacteristically slapped me on the back and lit his cigar.

"Jeez, that stinks Leonard!"

"Well, you know, Cuban cigars will become a lot better once we ban them. It's the forbidden factor."

Thanks to Leonard's cash stash I bought a nice suit in the style of the day. I then rejected it as trying too hard and went to Bonds and bought a sports jacket, a sweater with some random pattern and simple shoes. I stopped by a sporting goods store and couldn't resist buying some high-top sneakers. I hadn't seen Leonard all day but I knew that we would have to meet in the basement of Fayerweather the night after. Even in those days they turned off the boilers on Friday night, and so Friday night the two quantumnauts had to return to what we began calling "bubble zero." It didn't hurt that the gloomy rain forecast for the evening would turn into a full-blown soaker on Friday. Fewer people, fewer strange tunnel creepers.

I was so excited to see Elise that I walked up from 61st Street. I needed to expunge my nervous energy. The rain was only intermittent showers and I had brought a large umbrella, stolen from one of Ron's clients. I had decided on the sports jacket, a shirt and a sweater. If we were going down to the village, I assumed we'd have to dress like it. Elise and I agreed to eat at a small Italian restaurant near her apartment before we headed downtown.

I stood in front of her building and realized I had no idea how to get in. Then I saw a telephone handset. That was how buzzers worked in those days. I figured out that her apartment, 3G, I noted with glee, would be the buzzer code. "I'll be right down," she said into the handset. I decided to wait outside, trying to appear cool and collected. No ash cans, so no hiding place for Goldie.

As I was waiting I saw Joseph stride up. He didn't even notice me. He had an angry scowl and wore chinos with a button on the back. It seemed every hair on his blond crewcut stood up. He was only in a T-shirt. Not dressed appropriately for the weather. I was glad Joseph didn't see me. Confrontation and a bloody nose was one thing I was not looking forward to taking back to bubble zero.

Joseph picked up the handset and was about to dial when Elise walked down the steps and espied him. I shrunk back, not from fear but from some silly idea that I should give the young couple privacy. That meant that I was hovering about the entrance able to hear them, but not see them. Would Elise think I was a coward?

Elise wouldn't have to worry, she walked briskly past Joseph and saw me.

"There you are Pavel. I thought you had run away."

"What is this?" Joseph asked.

"A friend of mine, Joseph. He and I are going to take in some dinner, as if it is anything to you."

"You mean you dumped me for, for—" he looked at me and wrinkled his brow as if he smelled Goldie taking a shit, "for him? Jesus, you gotta be kidding me."

"Joseph, you know it was over long ago. We have nothing in common. Frankly, I wonder if the only reason you had me around was to do your homework. Which I am not doing any more. You will have to crack open a book now."

"I would rather crack open a head," he said, staring straight at me.

"Joseph, don't talk silly like that. Pavel is a friend, a friend of the family and that is all. But we're through, we're still through."

Joseph's bravado left him and he seemed to deflate. I imagined him as a giant balloon on a float after a parade.

"But I love you, you're like my princess. I cherish you. I gave you presents, I spent money on you." He sounded genuinely hurt and almost meek.

"Princess? Princess? Joseph, I am nobody's princess. Jeez, Joseph, you should really read more. Come on Pavel, let's go."

She took my hand in hers and we walked down the street.

"I should've known, you people always stick with your own kind. Fuck you, Elise. I don't need you and fuck you too Pablo or whatever the fuck you're called." I stopped, walked up to him. I was as tall as he was, even though he was all muscle and I was skinny and weak.

I edged towards him. Elise tugged me, "No, Pavel, don't. It doesn't matter." I had no plan. I slowly stepped up to him, got in real close. I could smell his breath, the burger he had for dinner. And I said, "Football, Joseph."

"What?"

"Football. One play you score a touchdown, the next play you don't. If you don't what do you do?"

"What the fuck are you talking about you skinny asshole, I

ought to..." and here he got really close to me, his dinner was a burger, plus the works, fries and I guess a beer or two.

"Joseph." Elise was tugging at me, saying "Pavel, please."

I whispered to Joseph, "Football, you don't make the play, what do you do? You punt, right?"

"Huh?"

"So punt. There's no harm in that. No disgrace. There will be other plays to score touchdowns, but this play is over. There are a million other girls in this city, easy ones. Go for it!"

I turned from him, fully expecting a blow to the head that would knock me out cold and perhaps prevent me from my rendezvous home.

Instead he just stood there. Elise and I turned, did not link arms, and walked away. I couldn't resist one last comment.

"Sunday, Chicago vs. the Giants, Chicago is going to win. Surprise."

"What an asshole! You don't even know anything about football."

But that was it, he did not pursue me in order to stomp me into the gutter. He didn't curse after us, we walked slowly away and he walked slowly away the other way.

Now Elise took my arm, "Wow, Pavel, that was so brave, a girl could feel secure with you."

"Well, I knew he was bluffing, guys like that usually are." Elise pecked me lightly on the cheek and said, "My hero, Pavel from India."

We walked silently and she said, "So are you going to tell me what you said to him."

I stopped and said, "You know, honestly, I don't even

remember. Truth be told I was so fucking scared." She laughed and grabbed me and kissed me hard.

We ate at a little Italian place called Basilicata. We quickly ran through our dinners and our wine, making small talk. Or rather she did most of the talking which was a relief to me.

"So tell me, my hero scientist from Bombay, this Leonard creep you know, you say he is a strange but smart chap, so why is he spending so much time in a physics for non-scientists course talking about Indian mythology?"

I was drunk too, and I laughed, "I could tell you but then I'd have to kill you. I am really a secret agent and I've been sent here on a mission."

"I half believe you, at least about the secret agent, but not about the killer part. You don't look like an assassin."

"The best assassins don't look like assassins," I said in a mock Bogart accent.

Our second bottle of wine, a shared panna cotta, and we were still talking, we were also holding hands and playing footsie. I noticed she was wearing a charm bracelet on her left wrist, with two charms: a Chai symbol and a yin-yang symbol.

"Where did you get that?" I said pointing to the yin-yang symbol.

From a friend of mine, this cool cat Claude, he's a musician from Martinique. I dropped her hand from my hand and she looked at me seriously.

"Does that really bother you that I am friends with a black man?"

"Of course not!" I said. Even for the fifties, I thought that was insulting. "You should know me better by now."

"Well..."

"Well, Elise, well he's..."

"Competition, and Joseph wasn't because Joseph is an idiot."

"Well, yeah, that's it."

We grew silent, the entire restaurant grew silent, our waiter presented me ceremoniously with the bill, I realized that it was almost closing time. The night had gone so fast but it looked like I had blown it. Oh well, that was all to the good, I can go back to bubble zero with a clearer conscience.

She excused herself to the ladies room and came back with fresh lipstick. She took out a cigarette and this time I picked up a matchbook and lit it for her. I gave an extravagant tip to the waiter and we left. It was too late to go downtown so I walked her back to her apartment. We walked one block and I stopped and held her by the shoulders. If Leonard could save Ronald's son from the racial strictures of the time, I could save a woman from the sexual strictures of the time. I said, "Elise, who do you really want to be?"

"What?"

"You know, you really can be anything. That's not just a pep talk. You, this, all of this, what we think of as reality is an illusion. It's malleable. You know that yin-yang symbol your ex-boyfriend gave you?"

"Friend, he's just a friend."

"Ok a friend, you know what it really means?"

"Of course I do, Pavel, I am not an idiot."

"That's just it, you're not, you're beautiful, and you're not an idiot. And your beauty? It's fucking meaningless because we all grow old and die one day. I'm gonna get bald and fat, you'll go grey and fat, and you know what, it is fucking meaningless, because our minds, your mind, my mind and all of our minds— what we hold in our heads, that is the only reality we can ever know. That is meaning. That is beauty."

"I believe you're drunk, professor."

I really thought I had blown it now.

"I don't know what I am saying, forgive me," I stammered.

She took her chin in my hands, looked up at me and said, "Follow the Tao."

We kissed, hard, passionately and then we walked the remaining blocks to her house kissing like that. It began to rain and I realized I forgot the umbrella at the restaurant. We quickly ducked under an awning on Amsterdam.

We kissed again and then just stood under the awning, her head resting on my shoulder, her eyes closed, my arm around her waist.

The rain let up and she said, "Pavel, what are you thinking?"

"Bohack has a special on rump steak, wow!"

She laughed and kissed me and I walked her to her apartment.

At her door she asked me in for a nightcap. "Don't get any ideas, young man, you just have to dry off."

We kissed and kissed again. The jazz on her hi-fi was Coltrane, which she said she hated. I recognized it, somehow we fell from her couch onto the floor, her shoes were off and her dress was halfway up her thighs revealing her nylon lines.

I slowly moved my hand up until I touched skin. She took my hand away and said "Back off, boy, but then kissed me passionately; she also put her hand on my privates, which were growing. We wrestled some more and I was on my back and she was on top of me. We dry humped a bit, her red hair all askew, dewy beads of sweat on her upper lip. She kissed me and took both my hands in hers, then said, "Close your eyes, promise." She began to unbutton my shirt and she kissed me on my chest and kissed me down to the top of my pants. She unbuckled my pants and took my now very erect penis in her mouth. Who knew there was oral sex in the fifties? She began to suck and lift the shaft and I was ready to explode almost instantly. She sensed that and pulled back, kissing me around my penis and then taking my penis in her mouth again.

I yelled "I'm coming," and came quickly. She continued sucking and biting on me until I was soft. She moved up and kissed me. I tasted the salty taste of my semen and her saliva.

We kissed some more and we lay side by side. I stroked her hair and looked into her eyes.

"You're beautiful, even though it doesn't matter," I laughed.

She looked at me seriously, "I hope you don't think I am some kind of tramp. I don't do that often, never with Joseph, never."

I put my fingers to her lips. "Don't worry, women should be allowed to express their sexuality as much as men," I said, mentally kicking myself for how clinical it sounded.

"Exactly," exclaimed Elise.

"Now, lie back," I said.

"No, I'm not ready, I don't have, I am not ready for that."

It was my turn to kiss her and pin her. I kissed her belly through her sweater and ran my hands up her hose. I quickly found the spot between her legs, and began to rub my hands there. No protestations, just soft coos and her hand running through my hair. I stopped at her skirt line and pulled her skirt down and off, surprising myself by how smoothly I did it. I kissed her leg, she wasn't stopping me. I unhooked her panties from the garter straps and slowly tugged on her girdle, kissing her by her belly button all the while rubbing between her legs through the fabric.

"Oh no," she whispered, "oh no..."

I stopped kissing her, but didn't stop rubbing her.

"We can stop if you want to." She kissed me.

I unrolled her girdle, because that was the only way I knew to get it off and then put my hand between her legs and felt the wetness. I ran my fingers through her pubic hair. She had a full luxuriant growth of hair with a small trail almost up to her belly button. Her hair was darker than her head hair but it was still reddish. I kissed her from her belly button down to the top of her pubic hair, now she helped me to get her girdle off all the way past her feet, and I went down further. I played with her pubes. I had forgotten that people thought pubic hair was normal in these times. I felt amazed by how much of a turn-on it was. I took one leg and lifted it over my shoulder and put my head down between her legs. I slowly licked around her lips, and then licked some more where her clit was, slowly at first, then in a more rhythmic way. I then went back to her lips and stuck my tongue into her vulva. I tasted the musky sweetness of her. I then went back to her clit. She climaxed and then it was my turn to kiss her, then I stuck my tongue inside her as far as I could get it, tasting her. I lay with my head in her lower abdomen and just took her pubic hair and made little dreadlocks with it. Then I kissed her or she kissed me.

"Pavel, no man has ever done that to me."

"Then that is a pity."

We kissed and fell asleep in each other's arms.

Morning came and she woke before me and woke me up.

"Come on, Pavel, you have to leave."

"Huh, what? Why?"

"My roommate will be home soon, she works nights, I can't let her see me with a man."

"OK, OK." I admit I was angry for being roused abruptly. I was expecting perhaps a morning repeat, but the franticness with which she was running around and throwing clothes got my attention. I got dressed quickly. She lit a cigarette. Neither of us had brushed our teeth.

"When will I see you?" I asked.

"Whenever you want."

"Well, perhaps this weekend," I said.

She sensed something in me, I couldn't tell her what.

"I actually have a lot of studying to do this weekend, maybe next week?"

"Yeah, maybe." I kissed her quickly, morning breath be damned, and walked out into the rain.

I took a subway down to 61st Street, crowded with wet commuters pushing and shoving. That part of New York wasn't different. I noticed the advertisement for Miss Subways, Wrigley's gum and Lucky Strike, plus Lifebuoy soap. I got out at the 66th Street station and walked to my lodgings.

I went into the house, past the red drapes and waiting customers, back into my room. There I saw Leonard conversing in hushed tones with Ronald. "You sure, you really sure?"

"Indeed I am young man. Listen, how do you think I know so much about you?"

Leonard looked up at me and said, "Ah, young man, I didn't think you would come back from your tryst with what's her name?"

"You know what her name is."

"Come to join the land of the living?"

"Is our work done here?"

Leonard looked at Ron and said, "Young man, our work is never done."

He then went into his room. I followed but from the left, behind see-through curtains of reddish lace, I saw a young boy looking a lot like Ronald, his head in a book. Curious, I stared towards the boy when Ronald said, "Why don't you join your friend."

RETURN TO BUBBLE ZERO

"I thought we were going tonight, under cover of rain and darkness?"

"No time to waste, young man, I want to leave, I am tired of this time, besides it is teeming out now, nobody will be on the streets. They are predicting a real autumn storm. Come on."

I missed Elise already and didn't like the way it had ended. But I wasn't unhappy about going back to our bubble. I needed an Elise in my life, but in *my* world. Maybe if I saw her, just saw her walking on campus, I would lose my nerve and stay. I could advance physics by fifty years. The thought popped into my head.

"Leonard, maybe this is how genius becomes genius. You know, Einstein pops into our quantum bubble from another, filled with knowledge already discovered. What is knowledge, but information?"

"Information observed and systematized by a human. Young man, I know where you are going, but then who taught the Einstein? No, sometimes genius is genius, and you my friend, while brilliant, will never be an Einstein, a Dirac, an Erdős. But you will have because of me..."

"An Erdős number of two, yeah I know."

I changed into the bland fifties-style suit I travelled down-bubble in—it is strange how Leonard and I are already coming up with jargon for time travel—and left my newly purchased threads on my bed. I felt someone, perhaps Ron, perhaps Ron's son who I'll bet is called Red, could use them. I wanted to be bland for upbubble travel.

"Time to go, young man," and as was usual with Leonard, we walked from 61st Street to Columbia, tempest be damned.

We snuck in through the southwest part of the campus, no security guards in these days and crawled through one of the tunnels towards Fayerweather. All clear. Leonard and I set up our Faraday cage from the metal sheets we had taken with us. We took out our computer, I noted with a chuckle that I got no bars. We entered the numbers, started the current, and voila!

Just like that we are back in my own time. I am in my office in engineering. Even the coffee cup with the Greek-style lettering spelling out "We are happy to serve you" is there, stained brown with no coffee. I realized that our absences needed to be explained—at least mine. Leonard comes and goes.

"Leonard, what am I going to tell Dave? I spent two days away without calling."

"Young man, we just successfully completed the single most important experiment of the twenty-first century and you care what your fancy-pants phony boss thinks? Don't worry about him; I'll take care of him. Cigar?"

And out from one of his inside pockets along with old newspapers he took two Cuban cigars.

"I stole them from the candy shop next to the luncheonette where we had breakfast yesterday. You can't get good Cuban stogies in this bubble."

"No thanks, I don't smoke. Plus, I thought you said that Cuban cigars were overrated, it was the forbidden aspect that made them so coveted."

"Well, I really don't know. A cigar is sometimes just a cigar, you know."

"Very funny."

"I have no idea what you mean," he snickered, and he lit both cigars and handed me one. I smoked a cigar for the first time in my life.

I snuffed out my cigar and handed it to Leonard. He made a shaking sign with his hand and said, "Keep it, young man, as a memento. Plus, it is Cuban. Forbidden on this campus, that is a mark of a cool cat."

"They don't say that nowadays."

"I wouldn't know, young man, so are you ready to write this up?"

"For publication? Shouldn't we keep it secret?"

"Certainly not for publication, not yet, but I will get you that Erdős number, but we have to write our preliminary results, maybe, you know, lab results, we have to replicate them, prove we..."

"Prove we weren't fucking hallucinating, right?"

"Well, yes, prove we weren't hallucinating, the, um... 'fucking,' as you call it, I will leave to you young Casanova."

"No fucking, just oral."

"You mean fell-at-ee-you."

"It's pronounced fell-ay-show. Fell-at-ee-you is ridiculous."

"Whatever, the genitalia is of no interest to me. It's dirty, disgusting, waste comes from that."

"Leonard," I began. Perhaps it was time to tell him to change his underwear and maybe wash his own genitalia, or wash in general, but as he stood there waiting for me, his white hair all askew, his eyes kind of bulging, his small pot-belly sticking out of the two buttons undone on his shirt, I decided not to.

"Nothing, well, um, thank you. That is all."

We heard footsteps but it was just Dave.

"Paul! There you are!" He looked the same, spoke with the same upper-crust accent, wore the same studied dressed down clothes, even his Chuck Taylor sneakers were the same.

"Paul, I've been looking all over for you, where the heck have you been? Don't you answer your phone? I should've known you'd be here with Leonard."

"Now, Mr. Chambliss, you should know that this boy was very sick."

"Leonard, let me explain," I said.

"Yes, Leonard, let the young man fight his own battles. This is very irregular. Thank God you had no classes to teach."

I looked at Leonard and looked at Dave.

"Well, Paul? Out with it."

"Well, um, I wasn't feeling well, you know...and, well, Leonard was helping me, after his breakthrough, I really think we can have quantum encoding at a distance. We just have to calibrate the lasers precisely. You don't even need a fancy Faraday cage because you don't have to shield one hundred percent. You know what Leonard and I found out?"

Leonard touched my hand gently.

"Mr. Chambliss, now you've been very generous to me. I am a custodian here, no longer an academic, but..."

"Oh, out with it Leonard, I want to help you."

"Well, I found him on the floor writhing in pain, vomit all over him. So I took him home."

"Why not to a hospital, you're not a professor, you're certainly not a doctor."

"Doctors are frauds, I haven't been to one in years."

"Why didn't you call, Paul?"

I jumped in, "I lost my phone when I passed out, it was covered in vomit."

"Well, you still could have used a land line. Old school, I know."

I continued, "Leonard and I got some work done, a good theoretical framework."

"That is wonderful, when can I see the results? And are you OK to teach? You are slated to fill in for an undergrad seminar tomorrow."

"Oh, fuck!" I sighed, I forgot about that seminar. "Yes, of course I will." I looked up to notice Dave blinking at me. He stammered uncomfortably. "Well, good then. You know, you aren't the best advertisement for vegetarianism. Maybe you should have a steak every now and then."

He turned and began to walk out and then stopped.

"Leonard, thanks. I always recognized genius beneath the layers of craziness."

Leonard and I sat for some minutes and we both said together, "He isn't cursing."

A fear welled up in me. I remember reading a short story in grade school, probably every kid read it—where they take time travellers back to the time of the dinosaurs. I don't remember the entire story but one guy gets scared and runs off and accidentally kills a dragonfly or a butterfly. They go back to the present and it's a fascist dictatorship.

"We're not in bubble zero, are we Leonard?"

"Well, probably not, young man, but frankly we probably can't get to bubble zero, ever."

"But we went missing, we went missing for the time that we were back in the fifties. How do you explain that?"

"Well, I really can't, young man, but if we are encoding information and using the device, so we are the information encoded and moved at a distance instantaneously, isn't it possible that our absence is information, and that our absence in quantum bubble two is encoded? It isn't like we ended up in a place where Hitler won. The differences are minute, they will have no effect on us, on who we are, none, it's as if an atom were moved just a picometre from where it was in our universe."

"But Davisson doesn't curse. That is fucking different. Butterfly effect Leonard, butterfly effect."

We walked out and we walked to my house, to my surprise Leonard stopped and said, "You go on home, I want to check on some things."

"Leonard, don't go to the lab. I'm serious. I'm scared."

"I promise, you go home young man."

I couldn't go home, I was too wired. I made my way to the Pear Tree. Who knows, maybe Red was a famous scientist. Everything looked the same. I was spooked. Dave cursed ostentatiously but surely a few sentences he utters must be curse-free. Maybe I was overreacting. I walked into the market. Red's stool was gone. The printed "In memoriam, Red" notice in all its Comic Sans glory was still by the counter. Red's still dead. The students were still the students I remembered, a buzz of ohmigods and cellphones and kids typing into their iPhones without even giving any notice to the real human beings taking their money and bagging their Ramen.

I walked home. The buildings looked just like I remember. On Amsterdam, a La Québécoise bus carrying Montreal sightseers ran a red light on its way back north from Saint John the Divine.

The next day in my office I was running through the numbers used in calibrating the lasers. I knew that with the redundancy we built in, we could encode pseudo-random information which contains real information in the photon patterns of the lasers. We did that. Problem solved. But then I realized that even with the redundancy we can't know precisely what is lost, what is changed, what is truly random. When we build a pattern we inevitably lose something. We can't be, are never, and will never be exactly the same. Thus it is absolutely impossible to go back to the same bubble. You can't go home to bubble zero again.

I also knew, however, that the likelihood of a Canadian bus transforming into a Das Hitler bus was practically zero. I think I could live with a curse-free Dave, but still fears lingered within me. We are messing with this bubble, and someone is messing with ours. I did feel better knowing that my life, at least my life in this bubble, wouldn't be like that short story. I made my way to the last block before my home and stopped. I realized that I was in front of Elise's building. I raced to the door, perhaps she still lives there, she'd be an old lady, but I had to see how she turned out. Of course, she never knew me. Maybe she married Claude, maybe she married Joseph and had two kids somewhere in New Jersey. I looked in the vestibule at the numbers for her apartment. The names were Xiang and Wu. Like almost all of the apartment houses in this neighbourhood it was a dorm for Columbia now.

"Wherever you are, Elise, I hope you had a great life," I said out loud to myself and walked home. Despite myself, I noticed licence plates. I scored an Idaho plate. It no longer said FAMOUS POTATOES.

The next day, I worked with Dave on the apparatus. Say what you want about Dave and his upper-crust upbringing, he was not afraid to get his hands dirty, not in this bubble or bubble zero. Since the smallest vibration could upset the lasers, we decided to encase the apparatus in vibration-absorbing foam. This meant that the apparatus was too large to fit into a suitcase, but I wasn't planning on being a quantumnaut anymore. A Philips head screwdriver slipped out of Dave's hand and he accidentally poked his other hand with it. "Fuck!" he shouted. I felt relieved. Finally a curse from Dr. Davisson Chambliss. Almost instantly he said, "Sorry, Paul."

"No problem, Dave, you practically stabbed yourself there. You OK?"

"Fine, but sorry for my language."

"Dave, I don't fucking care, you know. Everyone curses."

His face reddened. "Yes, I know Paul. But, well, it has become a cliché, especially amongst academics."

We worked silently that afternoon.

THE DIRTY THIRTIES

"Time for another trip." Leonard was speaking to me in my room. It was just like the first time he sat in my room like a roosting bat and began to convince me to become a quantumnaut. At least this time he didn't eat bagels and lox for breakfast. Actually, in this bubble, Leonard seemed to have had more of an attraction to soap bubbles. He actually bathed now and then. He didn't necessarily smell all nice, but having him in your apartment wasn't like having a homeless person who lived rough for the past decade in your apartment. He still didn't clean up his piss from the floor when he missed.

"Leonard, I'm not so sure. I mean, we don't know one hundred percent what the effects on us, or on any of our uses are when we traverse the bubbles. You know that story? Well..."

"Young man, nonsense, we are still ourselves and even if there are infinite versions of ourselves, we still exist. We'll never meet ourselves."

"What if we go back in time? We..."

"Can we what, kill our grandpappy? No, we can't. The younger self we see is not ourself, more like an identical twin of ourself at a different time. Just like an identical twin of ourself in a different space."

"What if we can't go home again? You know Red, that guy who used to sit in front of the Pear Tree."

"What about him?" I sensed a small catch in his voice.

"He really isn't from Georgia is he? He's Ron's son, isn't he?"

"What if he is?"

"You knew that?"

"No, I didn't until I came back. I never knew what happened to Red, he wasn't called Red back in those days. I don't know where the name came from. Once we travelled back, I..."

"Why did you want to go back to the fifties so bad? Was it to save Red, to save at least one Red?"

"No, young man, to save myself. I could've..."

"Leonard, if you say 'I coulda been a contender,' I swear I am leaving. Talk to me real. Drop the fucking act."

He stormed out. I didn't see him until the middle of December. So much the better. I was definitely not going back into the bubble matrix.

That December night I was in my lab. I had four energy bars and lots of coffee. It was sleeting out. The weatherman on TV called it sleet-pocolypse. I knew that people forgot that winters get cold in New York but in this bubble, at least, the panic over a little freezing rain was ridiculous, from the panic-buying of bread at the Pear Tree to the look of wonder on the faces of the students, many of whom were still not wearing coats. One would think palm trees lined the Manhattan streets.

The sleet did have one good effect. When the boiler kicked off, the semi-crystalline state of the sleet acted as a wonderful natural insulator. I took the lasers out of the foam to see how they would work. I encoded the information I wanted to encode. It was long. It was the story I had remembered, "A Sound of Thunder," by Ray Bradbury. I encoded the entire string with one laser and then set about the Aspect experiment, sending each photon in its pattern one by one. Even at the speed of light it would take some time. In a few hours, I would make a subtle change in the text and see if the error would be picked up instantaneously in the output.

It worked, the subtle changes I made to the source changed in the output—instantaneously. This was the best experiment yet and proof that we can direct spooky action at a distance. The best experiment, except for the one that was secret of course.

Despite myself, I googled "Elise Fein." I found a few entries, including one for a porn star who spelled Fein as Fyne, but none age-appropriate. Elise could've been dead. She could have married, maybe in this bubble she never existed. Maybe in this bubble she died because I broke her heart. I laughed out loud to myself. I allowed myself the possibility that Elise was the only woman whose heart I could break. Most of the time I was on the receiving end of that.

I was about to turn out the lights and leave when Leonard materialized. I was beginning to think that he himself was some sort of quantum strangeness. I never saw him just walk in but he always managed to come in. Given his legendary stink, it was amazing I never sniffed him before I saw him. I saw how wet he was with melting sleet and snow dripping from his coat onto the lab floor.

"Shit, Leonard, take your coat off get warm." He was shivering and looking worse for wear.

"Oh, young man, you don't want to hear it but I never coulda been a contender."

"What are you talking about?"

"I was at the library doing research, since you kicked me out of your office."

"Leonard, I didn't kick you out of anything, you walked out."

"No, you were right to do so. I realized I had to find out about Red, where I went wrong, what happened to Maria and Ron. You know what I found out?"

"What?"

"I found out that nothing I did had an effect. Ron killed Maria in '61, just like in our bubble. The tenements were torn down to make way for Lincoln Center, just like in our bubble, and Red went to live not with Maria's folks but with Ron's in..."

"Georgia, I know."

"Actually, I think it was North Carolina." He sighed and looked at me before he continued.

"But you see, young man, his mind, his mind that I tried to cultivate so tenderly was still lost to circumstances beyond his control. He was still beaten down by racism, his father, and his dead mother. Red was red in this world. Just like in this world, I am still me. I will never escape me."

"But the bubble we left, well, Red could've been someone there couldn't he have been?"

"Unlikely. We would have seen evidence of it. Bubbles are not that different."

We sat in silence. In my brain, I was trying to work out an idea of reciprocal conservation of information, sort of like a thermodynamic law, only for information across quantum bubbles. The sum of the information stays the same, only its state, i.e. reality, can change and can change only slightly.

Leonard said, "We need to go back, we need to see if we can control precisely, and I mean precisely what bubble we go into. Maybe we can collapse adjacent bubbles into one..."

"Bubble of probability so that we can go back to the exact bubble? But how the fuck will that work, the math is beyond me."

"Not beyond me, young man."

Leonard was off. I was tired. I slept.

When I woke up I saw the equations on the wall. They were beautiful. I still didn't know how this man, this old man who was a distinguished professor but now got paid to push brooms around, could work out complicated mathematical theories so quickly. Math is a young man's game and what would take me weeks took old Leonard hours. His proofs were like elegiac poems in ancient Greek.

"Leonard, this is beautiful but what are the practical implications?"

"We can control the bubbles, I know it."

"You said you can't go home again, that no matter what bubble we're in there is some small slight difference, an infinitude, you call it, of bubbles."

"Yes, but here, lookit! You use a probabilistic wave distribution to collapse the bubbles and encode the information and voila! You can get close to the infinitude you want."

It took a few minutes for the circuits of my brain to work through his gibberish. Leonard made up his own words for quantum effects but they were no sillier than "charmed" or "strange" for quarks once you inferred what they meant.

"Goddamn old man, you are right," I said in my best WASP Dave accent. "You are right. Erdős 2 is coming my way!"

"Young man, we have to try it, we have to go back."

"To 1958?"

"No, further, we have to go back far enough so that we get enough of a statistical probabilistic wave model."

"And no Elise to complicate things."

"Well, yes, it is time you started thinking with your head instead of that, thing."

"Leonard, you have a thing too, you know, you might want to try using it."

"A revolting thought."

"Yeah, it is," I snickered.

I told him I was not going to do it, that going back further was too dangerous. There were too many differences—too many chances to get caught. He didn't listen. On the appointed night, or rather morning, of mid-December we were going to be quantumnauts again.

"Leonard, how far back are we going?"

"A bit further than '58, young man, but your costume should suffice." I had on a baggy suit, formal shoes and a fedora. I thought I looked like a gangster from the set of *The Godfather*. All that was needed was a flower in my lapel.

Leonard entered the numbers. We called it the QPS coordinates I calibrated the lasers, put my hand-held computer inside my underwear—I wanted to make sure I could get back—and hit GO.

We were spat out on 116th Street but not the 116th Street we knew. This 116th Street was right in the middle of the campus where College Walk was today. It was very cold and snowing. Whatever quantum strangeness we brought with us, the warmer winters were not one of them. I was freezing even though Leonard advised me to bring a coat.

We crossed the street and out of the gloom I saw headlights coming toward us fast. I still hadn't got used to a thoroughfare across the Columbia campus. He honked at us and the horn sounded that old-time wah-HAH-hah I knew only from old movies. The car was a Model T of some sort. It was black with bicycle tires and sported a running board. "Idiots!" The man screamed. Some things didn't change.

We saw no one. The cold and the snow and early hours meant that we were alone. Both of us stared at each other, our breath coming out in blasts of steam.

"Leonard, I'm cold. Where are we, I mean, what time-space continuum are we in?"

"Hmm, I am not sure but judging by the pavement here and the car, I'd say we are in the thirties. Come, young man, let's walk."

And so we did, we walked down Broadway towards Columbus Circle. Few people were out which was just as good so that nobody noticed my astonished glare. I grew up in New York, the fifties Broadway was at least somewhat recognizable. You just had to ignore the fact that there were no condos. This Broadway was very different. It was mostly tenements and a few larger buildings. Some of the buildings are luxury in my New York, but all of them here looked dowdy. A few homeless people were sleeping on a subway grate with newspapers on top of them. Metal ash cans were filled to overflowing. Old cars that weren't old lined the streets. I heard the clip-clop of hooves and saw a milkman in a cart being pulled by a large horse who was taking a big shit on Broadway. A car, a more sporty old-time car, more like a luxurious sedan, sped down, honked and zoomed past the cart. The driver cursed in a European language I couldn't identify. I saw many "To Let" signs on boarded-up storefronts, but I did see a cigar store and luncheonette.

"Leonard, let's go in for a second, I'm cold, I'm tired, my feet are soaked."

"Mmm, maybe get you some galoshes, young man. When the stores open."

"Do you have any thirties money?"

"Actually, no..."

"I thought you had money squirrelled away all over campus."

"Ah yes, but I was a lad this time, I wasn't old enough to be a genius and horde cash."

"Leonard, what the fuck are we gonna do!"

"Keep your voice down, and stop cursing, you'll only draw attention to us. Listen, I have lots of fifties money. The money in the fifties didn't look so different from the money of the thirties. Nobody is going to check dates, trust me. The cash will pass inspection. Just don't use pennies."

I didn't like this but what was I going to do?

We walked into the luncheonette and I noticed the date on

the *New York Mirror*: December 17, 1937, along with a headline about Roosevelt doing something or other. A magazine had a cover story about Hitler's secret Jewish past, and the Japanese plan for Formosa.

We sat on two stools. "Wadda you'll have?" said the blond soda jerk who was in all white and had on a white paper cap.

"Hot cakes and toast for us and some hash browns on the side. And coffee."

Leonard ordered for both of us. When the pancakes came I asked for syrup. The man looked at me and plunked down a dirty mason jar of syrup.

"Gotta be real maple here, in these times, right?" I said to Leonard.

It was. The pancakes and syrup were delicious. I tasted the lumps in the pancakes where the cook hadn't mixed them perfectly. I tasted the pork fat in the potatoes. I didn't even mind that. The coffee was awful. Oh well, two out of three wasn't bad.

There were no more than three people here besides us on this nasty Sunday morning. A man sitting next to me was chain smoking and drinking coffee after coffee. His coat was dirty. He hadn't shaved and he had a grim set to his mouth. He was reading the *New York Daily News* sports section and circling bets to be placed on the horse races. He saw me glancing over at him and said, "Tough way to make money, but you do what you gotta do in dis woild."

"Yup," I answered. I had a feeling that laughing would not be the best idea but it was difficult to stifle a giggle. If accents in the fifties were stronger than contemporary New York, accents in the thirties were even stronger. Everyone talked like a stage gangster from a detective movie. I expected the soda jerk to pull out a gun, no, a *heater*, and scream, "You'll never catch me alive, copper!"

"Leonard, where are we going? What are we going to do?"

"What are we going to do? We will just be. We will observe, young man, that is what we are here to do."

We paid the bill with our fifties money, and Leonard was right. The soda jerk never looked at our coins. The total was so small we didn't even need bills. We caught a subway and took it to Brooklyn.

We were going to see Leonard as a child. I knew this and I knew that there was absolutely nothing I could do to stop it. I felt queasy suddenly, as cold as it was outside, that was how hot it was in the subway. Hot and stinky. Apparently all the unemployed who couldn't find a place to sleep slept on the subway—some things never change, but even the people who were on their way to work, frankly, stunk. Did nobody bathe in this era?

It was as if Leonard read my thoughts as he whispered to me, "They have other more pressing needs."

At the other end of the car there was a commotion. I heard a young girl scream. We pulled into the station and a terrified young black man ran out, a few white men made motion to run after him, but didn't. "What happened?" I turned to my seatmate, a tough-looking man with a many-times broken nose who looked like a longshoreman.

"Whaddaya tink? Dey should do here what dey do down sout I tell yah."

"Huh?"

"What, are you tick or sometin? I seen them do it all the

time. That coloured boy probably put his ting on dat goil's arm. Disgusting. I tell yah dey ain't civilized, dese people."

I saw the girl who was crying stop instantly. She then gave the man's wallet to her mother who smiled at her.

"Um, I think that girl just took that black kid's wallet. She caused the commotion."

"Whatevuh, I still tink we should be like down sout if you ask me." He went back to reading his *Daily News*.

At Times Square he got up and left. I whispered to Leonard, "God, what a shithole."

"Different times, young man, different times, and not good times."

Leonard seemed nervous. He had promised me he wouldn't interfere with his young self. I reminded him to keep to his promise.

We finally got out in Williamsburg.

"My god it looks the same, just the same!"

The Williamsburg of the thirties was filled with tenements with laundry hanging from them, old cars belching smoke, factories, a gas works, and on one side street, a dead horse. At least it was too cold for it to rot. The entire neighbourhood, even the entire city, was permeated with smoke. Smoke from factories, smoke from coal cellars, it left a grey-green sheen on everything. I had heard of London's "pea soupers" but didn't think that New York suffered the same affliction. We walked down one street to a corner luncheonette. A truck with lettering out of the old west sped past us. I noticed the driver had huge arms—power steering hadn't been invented yet, and he sported a handlebar moustache.

His truck was emblazoned with a hand-painted penguin and said "McGillicutty's Ice Service. To fit all needs." He was the icebox man. He stopped on the corner. I heard the parking break go up. He got out of his truck with a pair of tongs, grabbed a huge chunk of ice from the back and walked into a luncheonette on the corner. A few early riser kids ran after him.

"Come, let us go to that luncheonette."

"I just ate."

"Come, I need to show you who I was so you can understand who I am."

"Non-interference, remember?"

"Non-interference."

We walked in and Leonard was stunned.

"Young man, it is just like I remember it. Oh my God!"

There were racks of magazines in the front along with cigars and various kinds of candy. In the back was a soda fountain with a phone booth, an actual phone booth.

The Iceman came out from a back door and said to the proprietor, "Next week!" in a thick Irish brogue.

The owner returned the brief greeting with a thick Russian cum Yiddish accent. He then looked at us. He was short, balding, wore a vest and a dirty white apron around his vest. In a vest pocket he had a fountain pen and some paper. Even from here, and even though the vest was black, I could see the results of many leaks accrete on the vest corner pocket.

"*A gute morgen,*" Leonard said to the owner. The owner just nodded gruffly and went and got a broom to begin sweeping. Leonard and I were the only two customers in the place.

"Leonard, I didn't know you knew Yiddish."

"Of course, young man, Yiddish was the first language of every Jewish New Yorker in your parents' days."

The owner comes over, and in a Yiddish accent says, "Vot'll you hev?"

"Coffee for me and do you have apple pie?"

Leonard asks for an egg cream, extra syrup.

"Nickle extra."

"Vos is mit zayn schtellung?"

"Nit hock mir," then switching to English, "You vant or not?"

Leonard turns to me and says, "Mr. Schmeckman, mean old man. You know he lost his whole family in the Kishinev pogrom in '05. Speaks Russian but won't."

Mr. Schmeckman slams down my pie, without ice cream, even though I asked for ice cream, and slams down Leonard's egg cream. I don't think there was extra syrup.

The door opened and the little bells that jingle sounded and in walked a young boy, chubby, in black pants and a black jacket with outrageously huge galoshes. He also had on a dark brown beanie-type cap, only it has ear flaps. Despite the cold he wore no gloves.

Mr. Schmeckman hissed. "Don't mit di handele get schmutz over the magazines."

The young boy looked at Mr. Schmeckman and nodded. He looked at us and quickly looked away. I knew he expected us to yell at him, to make fun of him, to grab a magazine out of his hands. Surely life couldn't be so bad. Surely this kid had friends. Surely this kid was Leonard.

"Leonard, you fat bastard you tricked me. Non-interference my ass!"

"God, if I only knew then what I know now, if only."

"That's what we all say, Leonard. Nobody is immune from screwing up their lives totally."

"Ah but young man, I didn't screw up my life, I had it screwed up for me. The injustice. Just look at him. Look at me. So curious, so eager to learn. And how does that bastard Schmeckman treat him? How did his father treat him?"

"Leonard, lower your voice. We can't afford a scene."

"I'm sorry. I know there are people who were much worse off than me. I had cousins in Europe, in this bubble here at the time it is here, they are probably going off to school in Chernowitz. In six years in this bubble they are going off to die."

"Well, it's human nature to up-compare, I mean compare yourself to someone smarter or richer or prettier. It's hard to remember all the people less fortunate than you."

"Up-compare, I like that." But Leonard's smile was forced, or rather Leonard's smile was one that could not be forced so his attempt had the curious effect of having him talk out of the side of his mouth.

The young boy began to read a magazine: *Amazing Science Stories*. The cover promised an article on time travel and an interview with Niels Bohr. Pretty heady stuff for what looked like a seven-year-old.

Leonard swivelled his chair around.

"Do you like science, young fellah?" Leonard asked Leonard.

Young Leonard looked down and nodded. He put the magazine back and put his hands in his pockets. He began to count out change in pennies. He didn't have enough.

The boy quietly put the magazine on the rack and stepped

back. He perused some other magazine but came back to *Amazing Science Stories*. He glanced at Schmeckman and quickly took out the magazine and held it close.

"You're gonna steal that magazine, aren't you? Aren't you?" I whispered to Leonard, old Leonard.

The boy quickly begins to try to stuff it down his pants. Leonard, my Leonard distracts Mr. Schmeckman.

"What do I owe you Schmeckman?"

"How do you know my name? I never seen you here." The magazine falls out of young Leonard's pants.

Schmeckman turns to young Leonard.

"You! What are you doing? If I catch you wit a magazine, oh if I catch you, you ugly little runt!"

Leonard puts his hands on Schmeckman.

"Nit mit die kass. Zie is a shane boychick a khokhome boychik. Ich vil de magazine kauffn."

"Who are you?"

Leonard switches to Russian, *"Ya drook,"* then in English, "We are in the same boat Schmeckman."

Schmeckman looks astonished.

Leonard says to Leonard in English: "Young man, would you like that magazine? Please, Mr. Schmeckman, magazine for my young friend here and, hmm, how about some Baby Ruths? I know they're your favourite."

The boy, young Leonard, looks scared but nods.

Schmeckman grabs me by the wrist and says, his Yiddish accent suddenly gone, "I don't know who the hell you two are but an old man who buys a magazine for a strange boy is *a fagaleh* in my book, a queer. A poivoit."

"No, he's not, he's long-lost family. Trust me, let him buy the boy a magazine."

"I don't trust nobody." But he took our money, our fifties money without blinking and Leonard bestowed upon Leonard the *Amazing Science Stories*.

"Time travel my younger man, time travel is true. Drink from the fountain of knowledge."

Young Leonard ran from the store clutching his magazine, holding it across his chest.

We paid and left Mr. Schmeckman sweeping up behind us like we ourselves were trash.

After we left and were back out in the cold, bright, early morning sunshine I turned on Leonard.

"You said you wouldn't interfere. What the hell was that?"

"Young man, I stole that and got caught. Mr. Schmeckman tanned my hide good."

"What did your parents do?"

"Nothing, nothing…"

We walked on and he said, "I want to go home." I thought he meant our bubble, but he meant his childhood home.

We crossed a small park and we saw Leonard walking ahead of us. We saw three or four older boys walk into the park. Leonard looked down. The boys had knicker-type pants on and heavy coats. None of the boys wore gloves although some wore hats. They began to horse around and throw snowballs at each other. Screaming and shouting. Presently, a young boy picked up a rock, wrapped snow around it, packed it hard and threw it at young Leonard. It was a bull's eye. Leonard fell down and began to whimper. The boys were upon him. We were close enough to hear, but our presence didn't inhibit them in any way.

"Watcha got dere, Lenny?" One kid said and grabbed the science magazine from Leonard's hand.

"Gimme," Leonard pleaded.

Another kid kicked Leonard hard in the groin.

"Ain't ya parents taught you to share?"

"Gimme."

"Shaddup," another kid said and grabbed him. All of the kids pushed his face into a snowbank and began pummelling him. They rifled through his pockets. There were a few people besides us walking about on this frigid morning but nobody said anything.

"Leonard, I can't take it."

Leonard just stared at young Leonard getting the stuffing beat out of him, tears streaming from his cheeks. The pain of this was still real nearly eighty years on.

"Hey, stop that," I yelled, finally, and the kids scattered.

Leonard picked himself out of the snowbank and looked for his magazine. That was gone with the bullies. He looked for his hat and Baby Ruths. Also gone.

Young Leonard sat in the snow head down, shivering but making no effort to get up. Finally Leonard couldn't take it. He ran towards young Leonard.

"My boy," Leonard said as he picked up young Leonard and wrapped him in his arms. Young Leonard was absolutely petrified. I had never seen a child's eyes more agape.

"My boy," Leonard said, hugging Leonard.

"My boy, don't let those bullies get to you. They don't know you. You have in your head the elements of greatness."

Young Leonard was squirming, screaming, "Let me go!"

"Oh my boy, Leonard, listen to me. I know how you struggle every day. You think things won't change, but oh my boy, my beautiful boy, they will."

I ran towards Leonard, the people who were ignoring young Leonard were now watching us.

"Hey, put dat boy down before I call the cops." One man yelled. Leonard ignored him, and I tried to pull Leonard off of Leonard.

"Leonard, let's get the fuck out of here! They think we're child molesters or something."

"Go away, Paul!" He called me Paul.

"Leonard, please!"

I finally grab Leonard but Leonard is still holding Leonard's cheeks. "Oh *meine zindel*, remember you are a genius and your mind, nobody, nobody can take that away from you." Young Leonard breaks free and runs as fast as he can away from us. Leonard breaks from me and runs after him.

"Meine zindel meine zindel. Meine shayne zindel."

"Hey, stop that you fucking kike queer!" The man who first yelled is now running after us. "Why I aughtta..."

"Leonard, let's go!" He finally realizes the problem and we both start running. We both run to our left to fool the man but there is a crowd now. Men, and even some women, are running after us. I fully expect to die here in 1937.

We hear a whistle and a cop twirling a nightstick runs toward us. Soon there is another and another. Leonard trips, and I try to help him up but a young girl of about sixteen kicks me hard in the groin.

"Shame on you!" she yells. Soon after, pummels, kicks and punches greet us from all angles. Finally the cops break up the crowd, but one cop gives me a sharp crack across the kidneys with his billy club for good measure. I fell and was knocked into the snow, conscious but nearly senseless. I think I peed my pants but it was so cold that it froze.

The cops soon pull us both up and throw us in the back of a thirties style paddy wagon. "Youse is under arrest!" one yells. "Shame on the two of you. It's bad enough you do that to each oddah but to take a child." We are in the back of the van on our way to the local precinct.

We are paraded into the precinct. Luckily on a cold Sunday morning not much is taking place. The policeman marches us up to the desk sergeant who is sitting at a raised desk.

"What you got?" the sergeant says in an Irish accent.

"Deez two fellahs tried to, tried to... well, molest a young boy. Dere are witnesses."

"Freaks, eh? Put them in cell two." The sarge looks at us and says, "You had better hope God forgives your sins because your friends in the hoosegow won't."

We are pushed into a holding cell filled with two drunks, both sleeping in their own vomit. One white without any teeth and one a young black man wearing what I assume to be a fashionable suit.

Leonard looks dazed.

"Leonard, I'm scared. What the hell are we going to do? We have no ID, nobody to back up our story. And, frankly, from where I was standing, if I didn't know, I'd think you were trying to have your way with the kid—I mean, with you. How could you do that? You promised non-interference."

Leonard just stared ahead. He was tired, spent. Emptied out.

"Leonard, listen to me. We gotta come up with a plan. We gotta get out of here, back to our machine, leave. They think we're child molesters. Do you know what they do to child molesters in prison?"

A cop came in and opened up the cage. He kicked the drunken white guy.

"OK, Moran, time to go, time to go to work."

The Irish guy wakes up and sees the three of us. He walks out of the cell and asks to use the bathroom to clean up.

Soon the cop comes back for the both of us and marches us over to the desk sergeant for our statements.

"Name?" he barks to Leonard.

"Leonard Zavitsky."

"Occupation?"

"Janitor."

"Place of employment?"

"Columbia University."

The sergeant looks at him.

"Don't jerk me around, old man."

"It's true," I pipe up.

"I weren't asking you, now was I?"

After he was through with Leonard he started with me. I was scared, I had to come up with a good cover story.

"Name?"

"Pavel Feldman."

"Occupation?"

"Physicist."

"What?"

"Physicist, um scientist."

"Place of employment?"

"Columbia University."

He stares at me. "You know this man? You are a professor?"

"Yes, sir."

"And he's a custodian?"

"Yes, sir."

"ID?"

"Not on me, sir, no."

"So how do I know you are what you say. If you make a phone call you got anyone to vouch for you?"

I was silent, I imagine the rest of my life being behind bars subject to one indignity after another.

"Well..."

"Are you a protégé of him. They groom younger men, I know that."

I tried hard not to roll my eyes.

"No sir, he was just emotional, it is a family thing, he is related to the boy and hadn't seen him in years."

"All right, back in the cage."

A black policeman came into the station, unlocked the cell door, and took the black man out. They both stopped in front of the desk sargeant. I stared at him as a few of the white cops did. I didn't realize there were black cops in the thirties.

The Irish staff sergeant looked at the young black man quite gently and said, "Now, look here young fellah. We don't do these things around here. Now, this officer here, I know him. He's a credit to his race. He graciously signed you out and will vouch for you. We police see only blue, not white, not negro. Ain't dat right, boys? Now you do what he says, don't come around here, and stay out of trouble."

To the black cop he said, "Now, Tollie! Thanks for taking care of this."

It's just Leonard and me now.

Leonard stands up and moves towards the door, turning his back to the police.

"Young man, I am sorry, you don't know how sorry I am."

"Well, no worries. I know you are sorry you got us into this situation but you have to get us out."

"No, young man, that is not what I am sorry for. I have to go, I have to leave you. I have to save my young self." Just then I heard a sharp click and the door opened and Leonard was out. For an old man he ran surprisingly fast, zigging when the cop on the left zagged and zagging when the cop on the right zigged. Presently he was gone with two cops running after him.

I stood there astonished. A third policeman quickly closed the cage. He screamed at me, "Where is he goin'? Where is he goin'? Tell me you pansy Jew fucker or I swear I will beat you senseless."

I moved to the back of the cage. "I don't know, I really don't know! He is mad as a hatter."

I slowly lowered myself to the floor, half sitting in dried vomit. I was waiting for the first wallop of his nightstick.

"Zerilli, knock it off," the desk sergeant said.

"But, sarge—"

"Would you mind tellin' me how that fat old man got out of the cage and eluded three of New York's finest? Would you? How do you think the papers will write about it? How do you think headquarters is gonna react? We have an embarrassing situation here. We've got to correct it. Now Zerilli, this is what I want you to do."

Sarge and Zerilli conferred in whispers and Officer Zerilli left.

About an hour later he came back and spoke to Sarge. I needed to go to the bathroom badly but I didn't think that was something they cared about. If you had to go you just peed in your pants.

"Feldman?" The sergeant called this out very loud. I was the only prisoner in the cage so it seemed unnecessary.

"OK, Mr. Feldman, or whoever you are, we're releasing you. You can thank Officer Zerilli here. I ought to run you right through, you and that pansy friend of yours, but Zerilli interviewed the crowd, they all agreed he was the main poip and you even tried to stop him. We don't know where he ran off to but let's make a deal. You walk out and you keep silent about our lttle lapse in security here. What do you say?"

"Yes, sir."

"You're still young, you know, maybe you can get help with your, you know, condition. Stay the hell away from my precinct, if we see you back we won't be so accommodating." Zerilli grabbed me and with a hard shove I was out the front door and in the cold.

"Get the fuck on the train and out of my sight. You have five minutes."

I took the L across the Williamsburg bridge and took west side IRT up to Columbia. I had to beat Leonard in case he used our instruments to leave. I'd had enough of the thirties. I wanted out. I wanted Elise.

I knew right then that if I could go back to the fifties in a bubble close to Elise's I would.

The day warmed and the snow began melting into slush. My shoes were wet. I was tired. I got off at 110th Street and walked up Broadway to Columbia, and took a right on 116th Street to campus. I was a visitor here but there were no ID cards, I could just stroll into a laboratory. I went into engineering undetected. It was Sunday. I quickly made my way to one of the tunnels, expecting to see Leonard at every turn but there was no Leonard.

I found the suitcase, thank God, now all I needed was a power source as I set up my lasers. It took me the better part of a day to rig up the apparatus. It would either work or blow up.

I did the calculations on my hand-held. I wanted to make sure I got right to that November day or as close to it as possible. I hit GO.

I heard a boom and a loud crash but it worked. I assume I short-circuited all of Columbia in the thirties, but here I was in the fifties. My suit was old and worn, but I had money—a lot of it. I knew where Leonard squirrelled away cash and I began to traverse the tunnels. I located almost all his stashes. As angry as I was with the bastard I knew it wasn't fair to hurt this Leonard. I took only enough to make a start. I darted out onto campus. College Walk was right where it was. The day was a beautiful, warm November day. The honey locusts were in their mustard gold, some of the maples still had red leaves. Boys and girls were sunning themselves on College Walk. I knew I needed a shave, a shower and new clothes. I took to the tunnels again and went to Pupin on a hunch. There were still showers, from when this was nuclear engineering. Decontamination showers. I took a very fast one and dressed. Next, a shave. While I was dressing someone came in and barked, "Who are you?" I recognized that voice. Without turning my body, just my head, I said, "*Drook*, Leonard. *Ya drook*." Then in English, "See you at Ron's?" He stared open-mouthed and I ran as fast as I could. I went to Broadway where I had a quick shave and fashion advice from the Puerto Rican barber who marveled at my thirties-style suit. I had a good lunch and bought clothes. They didn't have what I wore the first time I met Elise, and I actually had no place to stay but I figured I'd go down to Ron's. I had a grey suit and a blue shirt, open collar, and a white sweater. I thought I looked vaguely European.

I quickly ran back to Columbia and sat on the Low library steps. A visiting scholar sunning himself in the afternoon. I spied Elise and Josie talking. I tried to inch my way closer without being conspicuous.

"Elise, I don't want to tell you what to do, but he is simply a dreamboat," the brunette said to the redhead.

"Yeah, I know, but he is an idiot." They both giggled. "I mean, he treats me like I am some girl from Long Island come to Barnard for a husband."

"Well, half the time I think that's what most of us girls *are* here for." More giggles.

I was back. I knew I would make it. I caught Elise's eye and smiled. They both giggled at me. I think Josie said I was kind of cute. I was confident. This was the life I was going to lead. I was going to make it, Elise was going to be my queen, no, my partner, in bed, out of it, in life!

I actually wasn't listening but I finally heard my cue.

"You there, man." Both Josie and Elise laugh.

"What are the Yankees doing today?"

"I have no idea," I replied. "I suppose out sailing their clippers or eating chowder."

They both laughed. Elise said, "Well, Josie, we have a man with a sense of humour."

She turned to me, "Elise Fein, and this is my friend Josephine Buxbaum, Josie for short."

"How do you do," I answered with a smile that I hope exuded an easy confidence.

Josie looked at me, "You weren't listening to us were you? It is all girl talk."

"Not listening at all, just enjoying the sun, it is a beautiful day, isn't it. Gorgeous for late autumn. Whatever it was that you ladies were talking about, I am sure it was interesting."

Elise looked at me. "You look so familiar, are you a student here?"

"No, I'm a post-doc in the physics department."

"Physics, do you know..."

"Leonard Zavitsky?" I asked helpfully.

"Yes, he is one queer duck."

"Strange but brilliant. I've learned more from him than any man alive."

"I hope you learned to bathe." Same old Leonard.

Josie left for her class, leaving just me and Elise. The conversation still flowed easily as Elise and I talked about physics for non-scientists, metaphysics, the *Bhagavad Gita*, time travel and the role of men and women. I was more infatuated with Elise—in this or any bubble—than I had ever been.

It grew dark. She said she had to go. I asked her, quite boldly for me, "When can I see you again?"

"Well, I have to break up with my boyfriend and he has these two tickets to a concert. Do you happen to like Pete Seeger?"

"Yes, I do actually."

"Great, meet me at seven at Lewisohn Stadium. Time's a wasting!"

I walked to a flophouse hotel not far from campus, quickly booked a room and walked up to Lewisohn Stadium, taking in the sights of my new home.

The concert was the same, the audience was the same. My infatuation only grew.

We went to the same Indian restaurant, probably still the only one in Manhattan, had the same conversation, played the same footsie. I walked her to her door.

"I've had a lovely time Pavel," she giggled, "you don't mind if I call you Pavel. It sounds so, international."

"Elise, you can call me anything as long as it is you calling."

She laughed. "You're so sweet."

"Can I see you again?"

"Well, I have some work to do."

"Tomorrow," I said, "I know it is sudden but I know a little Italian place around here, and then maybe after we can..."

She smiled, even winked.

"OK. My young professor." An awkward moment then I kissed her demurely on the cheek.

"Goodbye, Pavel," and with a breathy smile she was gone. Elation!

I wanted to get a good night's sleep and remember this day coming. The next morning I bought new clothes. I had a ready supply of cash and knew where to get more. "Fuck Leonard," I said to myself. "You screwed me in two quantum universes now? It is my turn to live and I'm gonna use it!"

It wasn't raining but rather was as nice as the day before. Oh well, the bubble was never a hundred percent the same. The rain will come. The awning will still be there. I felt I had to pay a courtesy call to Leonard, I knew it was risky but I did. I walked into engineering and asked for Leonard Zavitsky, physics.

Leonard, rumpled Leonard with dark hair rather than white came out. "Can I help you?" he asked and then stopped. "You, you, you're the man who was dressing in the showers. You spoke Russian. Are you a..."

"A spy? No, but can I have a minute of your time. You don't know me but, I know of you and your work. Erdős speaks so highly of you."

We chatted about physics. I told him I was a visiting post doc from Stanford and hinted that I would love to join the Columbia campus. I knew what he was probably working on at this point in his career, so I decided to help him with his research if only he put in a good word for me if I applied for a position.

"How do you know so much about my work?" he asked, "and why were you sneaking around the labs?"

"I'm an old friend from the future," I joked. "But please go through the numbers. I think it will help you solve the problem of spooky action at a distance, theoretically, of course. A new matrix model."

DENOUEMENT

The night was clouding up. I met Elise at her place. Elise came down in a beautiful black and white polka dot skirt that showed off her curves and her red hair.

"My God you are beautiful," I said.

"You think so? I thought you only cared about my mind," she said coquettishly.

"Well, that is what I was talking about of course!" I stammered as wittily as I could.

I was looking for Joseph. Our confrontation was late. I hinted at what happened with Joseph.

"Oh, he is probably pouting and licking his wounds, or more likely already looking for a sorority sister to try to undress."

I forgot about him as we walked to the restaurant. Dinner was delicious, our conversation was amazing. We talked until closing time, just like before.

"Walk me home, Pavel," Elise said.

Of course I did. She slipped her hand in mine.

"The night is so beautiful when it is like this, don't you think?"

"Mmm."

She stopped by the awning and suddenly asked, "Who are you, really?"

I almost doubled over as if I were kicked. "What do you mean?"

"Just that, who are you? Who am I? Do you ever think that we are just an illusion?"

I sighed a relieved sigh.

"God, I think of that all the time. Let me ask you, who are you really?"

"I am that I am."

"No, seriously."

"I don't know, Pavel, but when I am with you I feel, well I feel..."

Silence. The entire day led up to this moment but I couldn't do it. I waited.

"Well, goodnight Pavel."

There would be no nightcap unless I acted.

"Goodnight, Elise." She leaned forward for a peck on the cheek. I kissed her cheek and then I grabbed her and kissed her passionately, hard, so passionately.

She pulled away as if stung and opened her eyes and slapped me across the face hard. So hard I almost saw stars.

"I'm not that kind of a girl!" she shouted. And then said almost in tears, "I thought you were different." She quickly unlocked the door to her apartment and she was gone.

I had failed. I stood there. I stood there for a good ten minutes. Now it began to rain but I didn't give a damn. Finally I walked slowly to my cheap rented room, my new home. I realized just how much of an outsider I was in this bubble.

I was also an outsider in my original bubble, at home, even in Columbia. My entire life I've had this sense of walking past a bar or a restaurant where everyone is having a good time. The windows are fogged up. I clear the windows with my hands. I am looking in, knowing that nobody would invite me in. Perhaps in there was an Elise, but an Elise who didn't want me. It made no difference. In my bubble and now in this one, there is a hidden world, a network of friends and family and joy and life. Yet, for whatever reason, I feel like I am on the periphery. I remember that I used to peruse books of street life photographs from the fifties, sixties, or thirties. I was obsessed with them. I had a sort of unbearable longing to be in them, to be amongst the hippies in the East Village, or one of the zoot suited hepcats in the forties or even a Vespa-driving mod in England. But those were only photographs and here I was, a pathetic loner on the outside looking in. To me, "in" was represented by those photographs, or the friends I had no idea how to entertain, or the women whom I could only dream about.

I know, wherever I go, in whatever bubble I traverse, I will be an outsider, forever the wandering Jew, me and Leonard.

I had nothing better to do. Instead of my single room, I walked down to 61st Street in the pouring rain. I doubted anyone would notice me.

— END —

ABOUT THE AUTHOR

Craig Savel works as a web developer for a nonprofit organization that does much work in the developing world. His work takes him to interesting places and involves long plane rides where he entertains himself by making up stories that he never writes down. Craig is a former Jeopardy champion and New York native. He lives in Manhattan with his three friendly cats and his wife, Marion Stein, the writer. *Traversing Leonard* is his first novel.

A NOTE ON THE 3-DAY NOVEL CONTEST

It is no surprise that an idea as crazy as writing a novel in three days would arise from a province renowned more for its pot grow-ops, land-locked sea serpents and whacked-out politics. But culture building must be done, and so it was.

In 1977 a handful of restless Vancouver writers accepted the challenge to write a novel over the Canada Day long weekend. No one finished and no one was eager to expose their hasty efforts to the scrutiny of others. Yet, though there had been no offspring, a beast was born, and soon it arose again, demanding recognition and celebration of its existence.

In true pioneering spirit, the call went out, the gauntlet went down, and the 3-Day Novel Contest was on its way to becoming the cheeky and uncompromising rebel of literary forms that it is today. From its modest beginnings as a barroom challenge, it grew to attract the interest and support of neophyte and seasoned writers alike, from Canada, the U.S. and beyond. Now, nearly four decades later, it has become a unique contribution to world literary history and a put-your-keyboard-where-your-mouth-is rite of passage for hundreds of writers each year.

The contest has inspired the creation of thousands of novels, thirty-two of which have been deemed worthy of publication. From the inaugural winner, *Dr. Tin,* by Tom Walmsley, to the 2014-winning entry you hold in your hands, the winners of this notorious literary marathon have impressed both adjudicators and reviewers with their level of craft and accomplishment. Many other 3-day novels have been redeveloped by their authors to be later picked up by other publishing houses.

Over its history, the contest has found a home with a series of small publishers, including Pulp Press (1977-1991), Anvil Press (1992-2002) and Blue Lake Books. In 2004 a couple of Vancouver editors agreed to volunteer their time and effort to keeping the contest going as an independent organization under the name of 3-Day Books. In 2006 and 2009, the stakes of the contest got even higher for a select few during two seasons of BookTelevision's 3-Day Novel Contest reality series, in which a dozen of the contest's entrants wrote their novels under the public eye.

In 2012, the editors of *Geist* magazine stepped up to take over the administration of the contest, with Anvil Press once again taking on the publishing and distribution of the winning entry.

Throughout its history, the 3-Day Novel Contest has been called a "fad," an "idle threat," a "great way to overcome writer's block" and "a trial by deadline." Unconcerned, it continues to fly in the face of the notion that novels take eight years of angst to produce.

Get more information about the 3-Day Novel Contest history and rules at www.3daynovel.com.